6.00
pt

D1469074

Buttered Side Down

Buttered Side Down

Stories by Edna Ferber

Preface
by
John S. Bowman

Signature Press
EDITIONS

Signature Press Editions™

Published by World Publications Group, Inc.
140 Laurel Street
East Bridgewater, MA 02333
www.wrldpub.net

Published in 2007 by World Publications Group, Inc., with new preface.

ISBN 978-1-57215-470-4
ISBN 1-57215-470-5

Printed and bound in China by SNP Leefung Printers Limited

1 2 3 4 5   06 05 03 02

Contents

Preface

Edna Ferber? Short Stories? Most people under a certain age will say they have never heard of her—and even those who have will probably say they never knew she wrote short stories. Ironically, it is the latter age-group who might have more claim to pleading innocent: She is not generally known for short stories. But the fact is that many people of all ages actually do know something of Edna Ferber's work, even if they have never read a word of hers. One of her novels was the basis of one of the greatest American musicals of all time, and another of her novels was the source of a highly popular movie. And both these Ferber "spinoff" works are frequently revived and revered. The musical? *Show Boat.* The movie? *Giant.* Still not ring a bell? Never heard *Show Boat*'s immortal classic, *Ol' Man River*? And *Giant*—never saw Jimmy Dean's last movie?

For almost five decades, Edna Ferber was one of America's most beloved writers. Her novels consistently made the best-seller lists, and several others besides *Giant* were made into movies: *So Big, Cimarron, Saratoga Trunk* (also a musical, *Saratoga*). And not just a best seller: Her 1925 novel *So Big* won the Pulitzer Prize. She also co-authored several plays with George Kauffman, one of which at least is occasionally revived: *Dinner at Eight.* You might have even seen Edna herself portrayed by Lili Taylor in the 1994 movie, *Mrs. Parker and the Vicious Circle,* for Edna Ferber was one of those accepted into the Algonquin Round Table, that exclusive set of New York sophisticates. Yes, this lady from a small town in the Midwest once was quite a presence on the American literary stage.

So it is worth knowing more about her before taking up these short stories. She was born in 1885 in Kalamazoo, Michigan, but her family moved about until they settled in Appleton, Wisconsin, when she was twelve. She graduated from its high school and took some courses at Lawrence University there, but her family's finances did not allow her to continue at college. So having worked on her high school newspaper she got a job with the local newspaper, eventually moving on to the *Milwaukee Journal.* Her first published work (outside her journalism) was a short story in 1910, "The Homely Heroine"—included in the present collection. Her first novel, *Dawn O'Hara,* published in 1911 gained her enough recognition that she would continue to get one or another of her works published or produced almost every year for the next fifty years. Starting in the 1920s she would spend more and more of her time in New York City, although her financial success allowed her to travel pretty much as she pleased. When she died in 1968, the *New York Times* obituary observed that "she was among the best-read novelists in the nation, and critics of the 1920s and 1930s did not hesitate to call her the greatest American woman novelist of her day."

We shall return to those "critics of the 1920s and 1930s" in a moment, but for now we should mention that she never completely set aside her reportorial training. In the 1920s, for instance, after someone told her about the theater troupes that sailed up and down rivers presenting plays, she tracked down one in North Carolina and spent some time with the company to research what would become her 1926 novel, *Show Boat*. Three decades later, she spent time in Alaska to gain background for what would become her 1958 novel, *Ice Palace*. But for her many early stories involving stores and working-class young people she did not have to travel afar: Her father owned a general store in Appleton and she grew up in that world.

And this is the world portrayed in the stories published in 1912 in the collection at hand, *Buttered Side Down*. No one would ever claim they are major works of literature, but they are the kind of stories that should appeal to anyone who simply enjoys reading about people—fellow human beings caught in those situations that are not necessarily highly dramatic, let alone tragic, but which, in fact, mirror the lives most people live. It should also be said that they are set just far enough back in the past—the first decade of the 1900s, that is—to be both slightly "exotic" yet also still familiar. The clothing, the entertainment, the slang (a "gink" is someone regarded as foolish or contemptible)—yes, they may seem a bit "dated" but they are not so remote as to leave the reader adrift. As for the various allusions to individuals no longer recognized by most readers (e.g., Robert W. Chambers, Cleo de Merode, Maxine Elliott, Ben Brust)—well, we all know about googling.

Likewise, the occupations of some of the characters in the stories may not be ones that many readers today engage in, although, in fact, they are still the occupations of large numbers of fellow Americans. Many of the stories involve clerks in stores, traveling salesmen, waitresses—again, a world that Edna Ferber knew firsthand. Also social class plays a role in several of the stories, either explicitly or as an undercurrent: This, too, would have been a world that Edna Ferber knew growing up.

Of the twelve stories, two have men as the protagonists ("The Man Who Came Back," "Where the Car Turns at 18th"), one ("That Home-Town

Feeling") might be said to feature both the female and the male, but the other nine have women at the center. One might expect that in stories written by a woman and with women as the central characters, there would be a strong element of romance, even passionate love, and very likely marriage. In fact, not only do none of the relationships end in marriage—most of them end in thwarted love, or at least a relationship between the two principals that will not be consummated. As Ferber writes in her own foreword:

> "And so," the story writers used to say, "they lived happily ever after." Um-m-m—maybe....
> It is a great risk to take with one's book-children. These stories make no such promises. They stop just short of the phrase of the old story writers, and end truthfully, thus: And so they lived.

"And so they lived." No less, but no more. Presumably this is what she intended to signal to us by the collection's title, *Buttered Side Down*: We are often left standing with something less than the desirable outcome. This is what raises these stories above their somewhat "O. Henryish" plot twists. Do readers today even know what this refers to—the stories of a once greatly popular short story writer, William Sydney Porter, who used the pen name O. Henry? Publishing his short stories in magazines and books when Edna Ferber was still a young woman, he was famous for the plot twists that climaxed his tales. "The Gift of the Magi" perhaps remains the best known of these. That's the one about the young couple who find themselves impoverished at Christmas so the husband pawns his prized pocket watch to buy his wife a beautiful hair comb—and then discovers that she has sold her lovely long hair to buy him a watch fob.

True, Edna Ferber does end several of these stories with an unexpected surprise. And true, she does tend to embrace the good old-fashioned ways, the wholesome hometown values. But in general, her stories are more realistic—even tough-minded, one might say. Notice how several of the stories end with the female rejecting the offer of marriage.

But, yes, Ferber's fictions—her novels as well as her short stories—were designed to engage and entertain a large popular audience. Yet there was also something that elevated her work above pure pop fiction and probably it can be traced back to her own roots and childhood. For her family was Jewish, and she would later describe that it was not always easy growing up Jewish in the small midwestern towns where her family lived. Some of the anti-Semitism was simply a pervasive undercurrent, the country-club type, but some of was quite explicitly threatening. She evidently absorbed this and moved on and in general chose not to burden her fictions with the theme. (She did, however, deal quite openly with this in the first volume of her autobiography, *A Peculiar Treasure.)*

But the real point here is that Edna Ferber did carry over into her work her sympathy for minorities, for the underdog, for those pushed aside by the Great American Success Express. Undoubtedly her most daring instance was her decision to make Julie, in *Show Boat,* a mulatto, and in turn to treat her situation so sympathetically. It may be hard to believe it today, but at the time this was really quite brave on Edna Ferber's part. After all, she was not then the greatly popular and secure author she would become. Look, too, at how many of the stories in this collection feature individuals with characteristics that set them apart from the upbeat world that so many popular authors preferred. Lonely women, a homely woman, a newly released prisoner, and perhaps most striking of all, the young protagonist of "Where the Car Turns at 18th Street." This is the only one of these stories that could be called a tragedy, and it has arguably the most modern ring of them all.

For it must be admitted that in general these stories do not pass muster as modernist short stories. That is, they would not be accepted in the prestigious university writing programs and certainly not in the "classy" magazines such as the *New Yorker.* The verdict of those critics of the 1920s and 1930s—that Ferber was "the greatest American woman novelist of her day"—no longer holds. But before we dismiss her work as bygone pop fiction, consider that she did, in fact, employ a number of devices that now count not only as modern but even postmodern.

For example, there are her many "asides," mocking comments that undercut her own storyline—what postmoderns now describe as contributing to "the play element" in writing:

> Any one who has ever written for the magazines (nobody could devise a more sweeping opening; it includes the iceman who does a humorous article on the subject of his troubles, and the neglected wife next door, who journalizes) knows that a story the scene of which is not New York is merely junk.

> The women all liked Ted. Mrs. Dankworth, the dashing widow (why will widows persist in being dashing?), said that he was the only man in our town who knew how to wear a dress suit.

Birdie glided off to the kitchen. Authors are fond of the word "glide." But you can take it literally this time.

David, the Scone Man, was Scotch (I was going to add, d'ye ken, but I will not).

Then there is the self-referential element in several of these stories: she identifies herself as the author of the story to come—thus framing the story in the authorial presence. In "That Home-Town Feeling," she tells how she positions herself at a newsstand hoping to get subject matter for a story—which she does. In "The Homely Heroine," she goes one step further: She has herself being asked to write a particular kind of story by a shop clerk:

> "I wanted to tell you that I read that last story of yours," said Millie, sociably, when I had strolled over to her counter, "and I liked it, all but the heroine. She had an 'adorable throat' and hair that 'waved away from her white brow,' and eyes that 'now were blue and now gray.' Say, why don't you write a story about an ugly girl?" "My land!" protested I. "It's bad enough trying to make them accept my stories as it is. That last heroine was a raving beauty, but she came back eleven times before the editor of Blakely's succumbed to her charms."

She—clearly Edna Ferber speaking as Edna Ferber—then lays out her plan for the story to follow in a manner that is truly quite remarkable, mocking the very act of literary composition while reminding the reader that her work is just a fiction. Or consider this from the opening of "Maymeys from Cuba":

> To anticipate the delver into the past it may be stated that the plot of this one originally appeared in the Eternal Best Seller, under the heading, "He Asked You For Bread, and Ye Gave Him a Stone." There may be those who could not have traced my plagiarism to its source.

But enough of such defensive justifications. The plain fact is these stories are a good read. If they are a bit old-fashioned, they provide the gratification of looking through your grandparents' old photo album. What greater pleasure can there be?

John S. Bowman

March 1912
Foreword

"And so," the story writers used to say, "they lived happily ever after."

Um-m-m–maybe. After the glamour had worn off, and the glass slippers were worn out, did the Prince never find Cinderella's manner redolent of the kitchen hearth; and was it never necessary that he remind her to be more careful of her finger-nails and grammar? After Puss in Boots had won wealth and a wife for his young master did not that gentleman often fume with chagrin because the neighbors, perhaps, refused to call on the lady of the former poor miller's son?

It is a great risk to take with one's book-children. These stories make no such promises. They stop just short of the phrase of the old story writers, and end truthfully, thus: And so they lived.

E. F.

I

The Frog and the Puddle

A ny one who has ever written for the magazines (nobody could devise a more sweeping opening; it includes the iceman who does a humorous article on the subject of his troubles, and the neglected wife next door, who journalizes) knows that a story the scene of which is not New York is merely junk. Take Fifth Avenue as a framework, pad it out to five thousand words, and there you have the ideal short story.

Consequently I feel a certain timidity in confessing that I do not know Fifth Avenue from Hester Street when I see it, because I've never seen it. It has been said that from the latter to the former is a ten-year journey, from which I have gathered that they lie some miles apart. As for Forty-second Street, of which musical comedians carol, I know not if it be a fashionable shopping thoroughfare or a factory district.

A confession of this kind is not only good for the soul, but for the editor. It saves him the trouble of turning to page two. This is a story of Chicago, which is a first cousin of New York, although the two are not on chummy terms. It is a story of that part of Chicago which lies east of Dearborn Avenue and south of Division Street, and which may be called the Nottingham curtain district.

In the Nottingham curtain district every front parlor window is embellished with a "Rooms With or Without Board" sign. The curtains themselves have mellowed from their original department-store-basement-white to a rich, deep tone of Chicago smoke, which has the notorious London variety beaten by several shades. Block after block the two-story-and-basement houses stretch, all grimy and gritty and looking sadly down upon the five square feet of mangy grass forming the pitiful front yard of each. Now and then the monotonous line of front stoops is broken by an outjutting basement delicatessen shop. But not often. The Nottingham curtain district does not run heavily to delicacies. It is stronger on creamed cabbage and bread pudding.

Up in the third floor back at Mis' Buck's (elegant rooms $2.50 and up a week. Gents preferred) Gertie was brushing her hair for the night. One hundred strokes with a bristle brush. Anyone who reads the beauty column in the newspapers knows that. There was something heroic in the sight of Gertie brushing her hair one hundred strokes before going to bed at night. Only a woman could understand her doing it.

Gertie clerked downtown on State Street, in a gents' glove department. A gents' glove department requires careful dressing on the part of its clerks, and the manager, in selecting them, is particular about choosing "lookers," with especial attention to figure, hair, and finger nails. Gertie was a looker. Providence had taken care of that. But you cannot leave your hair and finger nails to Providence. They demand coaxing with a bristle brush and an orangewood stick.

Now clerking, as Gertie would tell you, is fierce on the feet. And when your feet are tired you are tired all over. Gertie's feet were tired every night. About eight-thirty she longed to peel off her clothes, drop them in a heap on the floor, and tumble, unbrushed, unwashed, unmanicured, into bed. She never did it.

Things had been particularly trying to-night. After washing out three handkerchiefs and pasting them with practised hand over the mirror, Gertie had taken off her shoes and discovered a hole the size of a silver quarter in the heel of her left stocking. Gertie had a country-bred horror of holey stockings. She darned the hole, yawning, her aching feet pressed against the smooth, cool leg of the iron bed. That done, she had had the colossal courage to wash her face, slap cold cream on it, and push back the cuticle around her nails.

Seated huddled on the side of her thin little iron bed, Gertie was brushing her hair bravely, counting the strokes somewhere in her sub-conscious mind and thinking busily all the while of something else. Her brush rose, fell, swept downward, rose, fell, rhythmically.

"Ninety-six, ninety-seven, ninety-eight, ninety— Oh, darn it! What's the use!" cried Gertie, and hurled the brush across the room with a crack.

She sat looking after it with wide, staring eyes until the brush blurred in with the faded red roses on the carpet. When she found it doing that she got up, wadded her hair viciously into a hard bun in the back instead of braiding it carefully as usual, crossed the room (it wasn't much of a trip), picked up the brush, and stood looking down at it, her under lip caught between her teeth. That is the humiliating part of losing your temper and throwing things. You have to come down to picking them up, anyway.

Her lip still held prisoner, Gertie tossed the brush on the bureau, fastened her nightgown at the throat with a safety pin, turned out the gas and crawled into bed.

Perhaps the hard bun at the back of her head kept her awake. She lay there with her eyes wide open and sleepless, staring into the darkness.

At midnight the Kid Next Door came in whistling, like one unused to boarding-house rules. Gertie liked him for that. At the head of the stairs he stopped whistling and came softly into his own third floor back just next to Gertie's. Gertie liked him for that, too.

The two rooms had been one in the fashionable days of the Nottingham curtain district, long before the advent of Mis' Buck. That thrifty lady, on coming into possession, had caused a flimsy partition to be run up, slicing the room in twain and doubling its rental.

Lying there Gertie could hear the Kid Next Door moving about getting ready for bed and humming "Every Little Movement Has a Meaning of Its Own" very lightly, under his breath. He polished his shoes briskly, and Gertie smiled there in the darkness of her own room in sympathy. Poor kid, he had his beauty struggles, too.

Gertie had never seen the Kid Next Door, although he had come four months ago. But she knew he wasn't a grouch, because he alternately whistled and sang off-key tenor while dressing in the morning. She had also discovered that his bed must run along the same wall against which her bed was pushed. Gertie told herself that there was something almost immodest about being able to hear him breathing as he slept. He had tumbled into bed with a little grunt of weariness.

Gertie lay there another hour, staring into the darkness. Then she began to cry softly, lying on her face with her head between her arms. The cold cream and the salt tears mingled and formed a slippery paste. Gertie wept on because she couldn't help it. The longer she wept the more difficult her sobs became, until finally they bordered on the hysterical. They filled her lungs until they ached and reached her throat with a force that jerked her head back.

"Rap-rap-rap!" sounded sharply from the head of her bed.

Gertie stopped sobbing, and her heart stopped beating. She lay tense and still, listening. Everyone knows that spooks rap three times at the head of one's bed. It's a regular high-sign with them.

"Rap-rap-rap!"

Gertie's skin became goose-flesh, and coldwater effects chased up and down her spine.

"What's your trouble in there?" demanded an unspooky voice so near that Gertie jumped. "Sick?"

It was the Kid Next Door.

"N-no, I'm not sick," faltered Gertie, her mouth close to the wall. Just then a belated sob that had stopped halfway when the raps began hustled on to join its sisters. It took Gertie by surprise, and brought prompt response from the other side of the wall.

"I'll bet I scared you green. I didn't mean to, but, on the square, if you're feeling sick, a little nip of brandy will set you up. Excuse my mentioning it, girlie, but I'd do the same for my sister. I hate like sin to hear a woman suffer like that, and, anyway, I don't know whether you're fourteen or forty, so it's perfectly respectable. I'll get the bottle and leave it outside your door."

"No you don't!" answered Gertie in a hollow voice, praying meanwhile that the woman in the room below might be sleeping. "I'm not sick, honestly I'm not. I'm just as much obliged, and I'm dead sorry I woke you up with my blubbering. I started out with the soft pedal on, but things got away from me. Can you hear me?"

"Like a phonograph. Sure you couldn't use a sip of brandy where it'd do the most good?"

"Sure."

"Well, then, cut out the weeps and get your beauty sleep, kid. He ain't worth sobbing over, anyway, believe me."

"He!" snorted Gertie indignantly. "You're cold. There never was anything in peg-tops that could make me carry on like the heroine of the Elsie series."

"Lost your job?"

"No such luck."

"Well, then, what in Sam Hill could make a woman—"

"Lonesome!" snapped Gertie. "And the floorwalker got fresh to-day. And I found two gray hairs to-night. And I'd give my next week's pay envelope to hear the double click that our front gate gives back home."

"Back home!" echoed the Kid Next Door in a dangerously loud voice. "Say, I want to talk to you. If you'll promise you won't get sore and think I'm fresh, I'll ask you a favor. Slip on a kimono and we'll sneak down to the front stoop and talk it over. I'm as wide awake as a chorus girl and twice as hungry. I've got two apples and a box of crackers. Are you on?"

Gertie snickered. "It isn't done in our best sets, but I'm on. I've got a can of sardines and an orange. I'll be ready in six minutes."

She was, too. She wiped off the cold cream and salt tears with a dry towel, did her hair in a schoolgirl braid and tied it with a big bow, and dressed herself in a black skirt and a baby blue dressing sacque. The Kid Next Door was waiting outside in the hall. His gray sweater covered a multitude of sartorial deficiencies. Gertie stared at him, and he stared at Gertie in the sickly blue light of the boarding-house hall, and it took her one-half of one second to discover that she liked his mouth, and his eyes, and the way his hair was mussed.

"Why, you're only a kid!" whispered the Kid Next Door, in surprise.

Gertie smothered a laugh. "You're not the first man that's been deceived by a pig-tail braid and a baby blue waist. I could locate those two gray hairs for you with my eyes shut and my feet in a sack. Come on, boy. These Robert W. Chambers situations make me nervous."

Many earnest young writers with a flow of adjectives and a passion for detail have attempted to describe the quiet of a great city at night, when a few million people within it are sleeping, or ought to be. They work in the clang of a distant owl car, and the roar of an occasional "L" train, and the hollow echo of the footsteps of the late passer-by. They go elaborately into description, and are strong on the brooding hush, but the thing has never been done satisfactorily.

Gertie, sitting on the front stoop at two in the morning, with her orange in one hand and the sardine can in the other, put it this way:

"If I was to hear a cricket chirp now, I'd screech. This isn't really quiet. It's like waiting for a cannon cracker to go off just before the fuse is burned down. The bang isn't there yet, but you hear it a hundred times in your mind before it happens."

"My name's Augustus G. Eddy," announced the Kid Next Door, solemnly. "Back home they always called me Gus. You peel that orange while I unroll the top of this sardine can. I'm guilty of having interrupted you in the middle of what the girls call a good cry, and I know you'll have to get it out of your system some way. Take a bite of apple and then wade right in and tell me what you're doing in this burg if you don't like it."

"This thing ought to have slow music," began Gertie. "It's pathetic. I came to Chicago from Beloit, Wisconsin, because I thought that little town was a lonesome hole for a vivacious creature like me. Lonesome! Listen while I laugh a low mirthless laugh. I didn't know anything about

17

the three-ply, double-barreled, extra heavy brand of lonesomeness that a big town like this can deal out. Talk about your desert wastes! They're sociable and snug compared to this. I know three-fourths of the people in Beloit, Wisconsin, by their first names. I've lived here six months and I'm not on informal terms with anybody except Teddy, the landlady's dog, and he's a trained rat-and-book-agent terrier, and not inclined to overfriendliness. When I clerked at the Enterprise Store in Beloit the women used to come in and ask for something we didn't carry just for an excuse to copy the way the lace yoke effects were planned in my shirtwaists. You ought to see the way those same shirtwaists stack up here. Why, boy, the lingerie waists that the other girls in my department wear make my best hand-tucked effort look like a simple English country blouse. They're so dripping with Irish crochet and real Val and Cluny insertions that it's a wonder the girls don't get stoop-shouldered carrying 'em around."

"Hold on a minute," commanded Gus. "This thing is uncanny. Our cases dovetail like the deductions in a detective story. Kneel here at my feet, little daughter, and I'll tell you the story of my sad young life. I'm no child of the city streets, either. Say, I came to this town because I thought there was a bigger field for me in Gents' Furnishings. Joke, what?"

But Gertie didn't smile. She gazed up at Gus, and Gus gazed down at her, and his fingers fiddled absently with the big bow at the end of her braid.

"And isn't there?" asked Gertie, sympathetically.

"Girlie, I haven't saved twelve dollars since I came. I'm no tightwad, and I don't believe in packing everything away into a white marble mausoleum, but still a gink kind of whispers to himself that some day he'll be furnishing up a kitchen pantry of his own."

"Oh!" said Gertie.

"And let me mention in passing," continued Gus, winding the ribbon bow around his finger, "that in the last hour or so that whisper has been swelling to a shout."

"Oh!" said Gertie again.

"You said it. But I couldn't buy a secondhand gas stove with what I've saved in the last half-year here. Back home they used to think I was a regular little village John Drew, I was so dressy. But here I look like a yokel on circus day compared to the other fellows in the store. All they need is a field glass strung over their shoulder to make them look like a clothing ad in the back of a popular magazine. Say, girlie, you've got the prettiest hair I've seen since I blew in here. Look at that braid! Thick as a rope! That's no relation to the piles of jute that the Flossies here stack on their heads. And shines! Like satin."

"It ought to," said Gertrude, wearily. "I brush it a hundred strokes every night. Sometimes I'm so beat that I fall asleep with my brush in the air. The manager won't stand for any romping curls or hooks-and-eyes that don't connect. It keeps me so busy being beautiful, and what the society writers call "well groomed,' that I don't have time to sew the buttons on my underclothes."

"But don't you get some amusement in the evening?" marveled Gus. "What was the matter with you and the other girls in the store? Can't you hit it off?"

"Me? No. I guess I was too woodsy for them. I went out with them a couple of times. I guess they're nice girls all right; but they've got what you call a broader way of looking at things than I have. Living in a little town all your life makes you narrow. These girls!—Well, maybe I'll get educated up to their plane some day, but—"

"No, you don't!" hissed Gus. "Not if I can help it."

"But you can't," replied Gertie, sweetly. "My, ain't this a grand night! Evenings like this I used to love to putter around the yard after supper, sprinkling the grass and weeding the radishes. I'm the greatest kid to fool around with a hose. And flowers! Say, they just grow for me. You ought to have seen my pansies and nasturtiums last summer."

The fingers of the Kid Next Door wandered until they found Gertie's. They clasped them.

"This thing just points one way, little one. It's just as plain as a path leading up to a cozy little three-room flat up here on the North Side somewhere. See it? With me and you married, and playing at housekeeping in a parlor and bedroom and kitchen? And both of us going down town to work in the morning just the same as we do now. Only not the same, either."

"Wake up, little boy," said Gertie, prying her fingers away from those other detaining ones. "I'd fit into a three-room flat like a whale in a kitchen sink. I'm going back to Beloit, Wisconsin. I've learned my lesson all right. There's a fellow there waiting for me. I used to think he was too slow. But say, he's got the nicest little painting and paper-hanging business you ever saw, and making money. He's secretary of the K. P.'s back home. They give some swell little dances during the winter, especially for the married members. In five years we'll own our home, with a vegetable garden in the back. I'm a little frog, and it's me for the puddle."

Gus stood up slowly. Gertie felt a little pang of compunction when she saw what a boy he was.

"I don't know when I've enjoyed a talk like this. I've heard about these dawn teas, but I never thought I'd go to one," she said.

"Good-night, girlie," interrupted Gus, abruptly. "It's the dreamless couch for mine. We've got a big sale on in tan and black seconds to-morrow."

II

The Man Who Came Back

There are two ways of doing battle against Disgrace. You may live it down; or you may run away from it and hide. The first method is heart-breaking, but sure. The second cannot be relied upon because of the uncomfortable way Disgrace has of turning up at your heels just when you think you have eluded her in the last town but one. Ted Terrill did not choose the first method. He had it thrust upon him. After Ted had served his term he came back home to visit his mother's grave, intending to take the next train out. He wore none of the prison pallor that you read about in books, because he had been shortstop on the penitentiary all-star baseball team, and famed for the dexterity with which he could grab up red-hot grounders. The storied lock step and the clipped hair effect also were missing. The superintendent of Ted's prison had been one of the reform kind. You never would have picked Ted for a criminal. He had none of those interesting phrenological bumps and depressions that usually are shown to such frank advantage in the Bertillon photographs. Ted had been assistant cashier in the Citizens' National Bank. In a mad moment he had attempted a little sleight-of-hand act in which certain Citizens' National funds were to be transformed into certain glittering shares and back again so quickly that the examiners couldn't follow it with their eyes. But Ted was unaccustomed to these now-you-see-it-and-now-you-don't feats and his hand slipped. The trick dropped to the floor with an awful clatter.

Ted had been a lovable young kid, six feet high, and blonde, with a great reputation as a dresser. He had the first yellow plush hat in our town. It sat on his golden head like a halo. The women all liked Ted. Mrs. Dankworth, the dashing widow (why will widows persist in being dashing?), said that he was the only man in our town who knew how to wear a dress suit. The men were forever slapping him on the back and asking him to have a little something. Ted's good looks and his clever tongue and a certain charming Irish way he had with him caused him to be taken up by the smart set. Now, if you've never lived in a small town you will be much amused at the idea of its boasting a smart set. Which proves your ignorance. The small town smart set is deadly serious about its smartness. It likes to take six-hour runs down to the city to fit a pair of shoes and hear Caruso. Its clothes are as well made, and its scandals as crisp, and its pace as hasty, and its golf club as dull as the clothes, and scandals, and pace, and golf club of its city cousins.

The hasty pace killed Ted. He tried to keep step in a set of young folks whose fathers had made our town. And all the time his pocketbook was yelling, "Whoa!" The young people ran largely to scarlet-upholstered touring cars, and country-club doings, and house parties, as small town younger generations are apt to. When Ted went to high school half the boys in his little clique spent their after-school hours dashing up and down Main street in their big, glittering cars, sitting slumped down on the middle of their spines in front of the steering wheel, their sleeves rolled up, their hair combed a militant pompadour. One or the other of them always took Ted along. It is fearfully easy to develop a taste for that kind of thing. As he grew older, the taste took root and became a habit.

Ted came out after serving his term, still handsome, in spite of all that story-writers may have taught to the contrary. But we'll make this concession to the old tradition. There was a difference.

His radiant blondeur was dimmed in some intangible, elusive way. Birdie Callahan, who had worked in Ted's mother's kitchen for years, and who had gone back to her old job at the Haley House after her mistress's death, put it sadly, thus:

"He was always th' han'some divil. I used to look forward to ironin' day just for the pleasure of pressin' his fancy shirts for him. I'm that partial to them swell blondes. But I dinnaw, he's changed. Doin' time has taken the edge off his hair an' complexion. Not changed his color, do yuh mind, but dulled it, like a gold ring, or the like, that has tarnished."

Ted was seated in the smoker, with a chip on his shoulder, and a sick horror of encountering some one he knew in his heart, when Jo Haley, of the Haley House, got on at Westport, homeward bound. Jo Haley is the most eligible bachelor in our town, and the slipperiest. He has made the Haley House a gem, so that traveling men will cut half a dozen towns to Sunday there. If he should say "Jump through this!" to any girl in our town she'd jump.

Jo Haley strolled leisurely up the car aisle toward Ted. Ted saw him coming and sat very still, waiting.

"Hello, Ted! How's Ted?" said Jo Haley, casually. And dropped into the adjoining seat without any more fuss.

Ted wet his lips slightly and tried to say something. He had been a breezy talker. But the words would not come. Jo Haley made no effort to cover the situation with a rush of conversation. He did not seem to realize that there was any situation to cover. He champed the end of his cigar and handed one to Ted.

"Well, you've taken your lickin', kid. What you going to do now?"

The rawness of it made Ted wince. "Oh, I don't know," he stammered. "I've a job half promised in Chicago."

"What doing?"

Ted laughed a short and ugly laugh. "Driving a brewery auto truck."

Jo Haley tossed his cigar dexterously to the opposite corner of his mouth and squinted thoughtfully along its bulging sides.

"Remember that Wenzel girl that's kept books for me for the last six years? She's leaving in a couple of months to marry a New York guy that travels for ladies' cloaks and suits. After she goes it's nix with the lady bookkeepers for me. Not that Minnie isn't a good, straight girl, and honest, but no girl can keep books with one eye on a column of figures and the other on a traveling man in a brown suit and a red necktie, unless she's cross-eyed, and you bet Minnie ain't. The job's yours if you want it. Eighty a month to start on, and board."

"I—can't, Jo. Thanks just the same. I'm going to try to begin all over again, somewhere else, where nobody knows me."

"Oh yes," said Jo. "I knew a fellow that did that. After he came out he grew a beard, and wore eyeglasses, and changed his name. Had a quick, crisp way of talkin', and he cultivated a drawl and went west and started in business. Real estate, I think. Anyway, the second month he was there in walks a fool he used to know and bellows: "Why if it ain't Bill! Hello, Bill! I thought you was doing time yet.' That was enough. Ted, you can black your face, and dye your hair, and squint, and some fine day, sooner or later, somebody'll come along and blab the whole thing. And say, the older it gets the worse it sounds, when it does come out. Stick around here where you grew up, Ted."

Ted clasped and unclasped his hands uncomfortably. "I can't figure out why you should care how I finish."

"No reason," answered Jo. "Not a darned one. I wasn't ever in love with your ma, like the guy on the stage; and I never owed your pa a cent. So it ain't a guilty conscience. I guess it's just pure cussedness, and a hankerin' for a new investment. I'm curious to know how'll you turn out. You've got the makin's of what the newspapers call a Leading Citizen, even if you did fall down once. If I'd ever had time to get married, which I never will have, a first-class hotel bein' more worry and expense than a Pittsburg steel magnate's whole harem, I'd have wanted somebody to do the same for my kid. That sounds slushy, but it's straight."

"I don't seem to know how to thank you," began Ted, a little husky as to voice.

"Call around to-morrow morning," interrupted Jo Haley, briskly, "and Minnie Wenzel will show you the ropes. You and her can work together for a couple of months. After then she's leaving to make her underwear, and that. I should think she'd have a bale of it by this time. Been embroidering them shimmy things and lunch cloths back of the desk when she thought I wasn't lookin' for the last six months."

Ted came down next morning at 8 A.M. with his nerve between his teeth and the chip still balanced lightly on his shoulder. Five minutes later Minnie Wenzel knocked it off. When Jo Haley introduced the two jocularly, knowing that they had originally met in the First Reader room, Miss Wenzel acknowledged the introduction icily by lifting her left eyebrow slightly and drawing down the corners of her mouth. Her air of hauteur was a triumph, considering that she was handicapped by black sateen sleevelets.

I wonder how one could best describe Miss Wenzel? There is one of her in every small town. Let me think (business of hand on brow). Well, she always paid eight dollars for her corsets when most girls in a similar position got theirs for fifty-nine cents in the basement. Nature had been kind to her. The hair that had been a muddy brown in Minnie's school-girl days it had touched with a magic red-gold wand. Birdie Callahan always said that Minnie was working only to wear out her old clothes.

After the introduction Miss Wenzel followed Jo Haley into the lobby. She took no pains to lower her voice.

"Well, I must say, Mr. Haley, you've got a fine nerve! If my gentleman friend was to hear of my working with an ex-con I wouldn't be surprised if he'd break off the engagement. I should think you'd have some respect for the feelings of a lady with a name to keep up, and engaged to a swell fellow like Mr. Schwartz."

"Say, listen, m' girl," replied Jo Haley. "The law don't cover all the tricks. But if stuffing an order was a criminal offense I'll bet your swell traveling man would be doing a life term."

Ted worked that day with his teeth set so that his jaws ached next morning. Minnie Wenzel spoke to him only when necessary and then in terms of dollars and cents. When dinner time came she divested herself of the black sateen sleevelets, wriggled from the shoulders down a la Patricia O'Brien, produced a chamois skin, and disappeared in the direction of the washroom. Ted waited until the dining-room was almost deserted. Then he went in to dinner alone. Some one in white wearing an absurd little pocket handkerchief of an apron led him to a seat in a far corner of the big room. Ted did not lift his eyes higher than the snowy square of the apron. The Apron drew out a chair, shoved it under Ted's knees in the way Aprons have, and thrust a printed menu at him.

"Roast beef, medium," said Ted, without looking up.

"Bless your heart, yuh ain't changed a bit. I remember how yuh used to jaw when it was too well done," said the Apron, fondly.

Ted's head came up with a jerk.

"So yuh will cut yer old friends, is it?" grinned Birdie Callahan. "If this wasn't a public dining-room maybe yuh'd shake hands with a poor but proud workin' girrul. Yer as good lookin' a divil as ever, Mister Ted."

Ted's hand shot out and grasped hers. "Birdie! I could weep on your apron! I never was so glad to see any one in my life. Just to look at you makes me homesick. What in Sam Hill are you doing here?"

"Waitin'. After yer ma died, seemed like I didn't care t' work fer no other privit fam'ly, so I came back here on my old job. I'll bet I'm the homeliest head waitress in captivity."

Ted's nervous fingers were pleating the tablecloth. His voice sank to a whisper. "Birdie, tell me the God's truth. Did those three years cause her death?"

"Niver!" lied Birdie. "I was with her to the end. It started with a cold on th' chest. Have some French fried with yer beef, Mr. Teddy. They're illigent to-day."

Birdie glided off to the kitchen. Authors are fond of the word "glide." But you can take it literally this time. Birdie had a face that looked like a huge mistake, but she walked like a panther, and they're said to be the last cry as gliders. She walked with her chin up and her hips firm. That comes from juggling trays. You have to walk like that to keep your nose out of the soup. After a while the walk becomes a habit. Any seasoned dining-room girl could give lessons in walking to the Delsarte teacher of an Eastern finishing school.

From the day that Birdie Callahan served Ted with the roast beef medium and the elegant French fried, she appointed herself monitor over his food and clothes and morals. I wish I could find words to describe his bitter loneliness. He did not seek companionship. The men, although not directly avoiding him, seemed somehow to have pressing business whenever they happened in his vicinity. The women ignored him. Mrs. Dankworth, still dashing and still widowed, passed Ted one day and looked fixedly at a point one inch above his head. In a town like ours the Haley House is like a big, hospitable clubhouse. The men drop in there the first thing in the morning, and the last thing at night, to hear the gossip and buy a cigar and jolly the girl at the cigar counter. Ted spoke to them when they spoke to him. He began to develop a certain grim line about the mouth. Jo Haley watched him from afar, and the longer he watched the kinder and more speculative grew the look in his eyes. And slowly and surely there grew in the hearts of our townspeople a certain new respect and admiration for this boy who was fighting his fight.

Ted got into the habit of taking his meals late, so that Birdie Callahan could take the time to talk to him.

"Birdie," he said one day, when she brought his soup, "do you know that you're the only decent woman who'll talk to me? Do you know what I mean when I say that I'd give the rest of my life if I could just put my head in my mother's lap and have her muss up my hair and call me foolish names?"

Birdie Callahan cleared her throat and said abruptly: "I was noticin' yesterday your gray pants needs pressin' bad. Bring 'em down tomorrow mornin' and I'll give 'em th' elegant crease in the laundry."

So the first weeks went by, and the two months of Miss Wenzel's stay came to an end. Ted thanked his God and tried hard not to wish that she was a man so that he could punch her head.

The day before the time appointed for her departure she was closeted with Jo Haley for a long, long time. When finally she emerged a bellboy lounged up to Ted with a message.

"Wenzel says th' Old Man wants t' see you. 'S in his office. Say, Mr. Terrill, do yuh think they can play to-day? It's pretty wet."

Jo Haley was sunk in the depths of his big leather chair. He did not look up as Ted entered. "Sit down," he said. Ted sat down and waited, puzzled.

"As a wizard at figures," mused Jo Haley at last, softly as though to himself, "I'm a frost. A column of figures on paper makes my head swim.

But I can carry a whole regiment of 'em in my head. I know every time the barkeeper draws one in the dark. I've been watchin' this thing for the last two weeks hopin' you'd quit and come and tell me." He turned suddenly and faced Ted. "Ted, old kid," he said sadly, "what'n'ell made you do it again?"

"What's the joke?" asked Ted.

"Now, Ted," remonstrated Jo Haley, "that way of talkin' won't help matters none. As I said, I'm rotten at figures. But you're the first investment that ever turned out bad, and let me tell you I've handled some mighty bad smelling ones. Why, kid, if you had just come to me on the quiet and asked for the loan of a hundred or so why—"

"What's the joke, Jo?" said Ted again, slowly.

"This ain't my notion of a joke," came the terse answer. "We're three hundred short."

The last vestige of Ted Terrill's old-time radiance seemed to flicker and die, leaving him ashen and old.

"Short?" he repeated. Then, "My God!" in a strangely colorless voice—"My God!" He looked down at his fingers impersonally, as though they belonged to some one else. Then his hand clutched Jo Haley's arm with the grip of fear. "Jo! Jo! That's the thing that has haunted me day and night, till my nerves are raw. The fear of doing it again. Don't laugh at me, will you? I used to lie awake nights going over that cursed business of the bank—over and over—till the cold sweat would break out all over me. I used to figure it all out again, step by step, until—Jo, could a man steal and not know it? Could thinking of a thing like that drive a man crazy? Because if it could—if it could—then—"

"I don't know," said Jo Haley, "but it sounds darned fishy." He had a hand on Ted's shaking shoulder, and was looking into the white, drawn face. "I had great plans for you, Ted. But Minnie Wenzel's got it all down on slips of paper. I might as well call her in again, and we'll have the whole blamed thing out."

Minnie Wenzel came. In her hand were slips of paper, and books with figures in them, and Ted looked and saw things written in his own hand that should not have been there. And he covered his shamed face with his two hands and gave thanks that his mother was dead.

There came three sharp raps at the office door. The tense figures within jumped nervously.

"Keep out!" called Jo Haley, "whoever you are." Whereupon the door opened and Birdie Callahan breezed in.

"Get out, Birdie Callahan," roared Jo. "You're in the wrong pew."

Birdie closed the door behind her composedly and came farther into the room. "Pete th' pasthry cook just tells me that Minnie Wenzel told th' day clerk, who told the barkeep, who told th' janitor, who told th' chef, who told Pete, that Minnie had caught Ted stealin' some three hundred dollars."

Ted took a quick step forward. "Birdie, for Heaven's sake keep out of this. You can't make things any better. You may believe in me, but—"

"Where's the money?" asked Birdie.

Ted stared at her a moment, his mouth open ludicrously.

"Why—I—don't—know," he articulated, painfully. "I never thought of that."

Birdie snorted defiantly. "I thought so. D'ye know," sociably, "I was visitin' with my aunt Mis' Mulcahy last evenin'."

There was a quick rustle of silks from Minnie Wenzel's direction.

"Say, look here—" began Jo Haley, impatiently.

"Shut up, Jo Haley!" snapped Birdie. "As I was sayin', I was visitin' with my aunt Mis' Mulcahy. She does fancy washin' an' ironin' for the swells. An' Minnie Wenzel, there bein' none sweller, hires her to do up her weddin' linens. Such smears av hand embridery an' Irish crochet she never see th' likes, Mis' Mulcahy says, and she's seen a lot. And as a special treat to the poor owld soul, why Minnie Wenzel lets her see some av her weddin' clo'es. There never yet was a woman who cud resist showin' her weddin' things to every other woman she cud lay hands on. Well, Mis' Mulcahy, she see that grand trewsow and she said she never saw th' beat. Dresses! Well, her going away suit alone comes to eighty dollars, for it's bein' made by Molkowsky, the little Polish tailor. An' her weddin' dress is satin, do yuh mind! Oh, it was a real treat for my aunt Mis' Mulcahy."

Birdie walked over to where Minnie Wenzel sat, very white and still, and pointed a stubby red finger in her face. "'Tis the grand manager ye are, Miss Wenzel, gettin' satins an' tailor-mades on yer salary. It takes a woman, Minnie Wenzel, to see through a woman's thricks."

"Well I'll be dinged!" exploded Jo Haley.

"Yuh'd better be!" retorted Birdie Callahan.

Minnie Wenzel stood up, her lip caught between her teeth.

"Am I to understand, Jo Haley, that you dare to accuse me of taking your filthy money, instead of that miserable ex-con there who has done time?"

"That'll do, Minnie," said Jo Haley, gently. "That's a-plenty."

"Prove it," went on Minnie, and then looked as though she wished she hadn't.

"A business college edjication is a grand foine thing," observed Birdie. "Miss Wenzel is a graduate av wan. They teach you everything from drawin' birds with tail feathers to plain and fancy penmanship. In fact, they teach everything in the writin' line except forgery, an' I ain't so sure they haven't got a coorse in that."

"I don't care," whimpered Minnie Wenzel suddenly, sinking in a limp heap on the floor. "I had to do it. I'm marrying a swell fellow and a girl's got to have some clothes that don't look like a Bird Center dress-maker's work. He's got three sisters. I saw their pictures and they're coming to the wedding. They're the kind that wear low-necked dresses in the evening, and have their hair and nails done downtown. I haven't got a thing but my looks. Could I go to New York dressed like a rube? On the square, Jo, I worked here six years and never took a sou. But things got away from me. The tailor wouldn't finish my suit unless I paid him fifty dollars down. I only took fifty at first, intending to pay it back. Honest to goodness, Jo, I did."

"Cut it out," said Jo Haley, "and get up. I was going to give you a check for your wedding, though I hadn't counted on no three hundred. We'll call it square. And I hope you'll be happy, but I don't gamble on it. You'll be goin' through your man's pants pockets before you're married a year. You can take your hat and fade. I'd like to know how I'm ever going to square this thing with Ted and Birdie."

"An' me standin' here gassin' while them fool girls in the dinin'-room can't set a table decent, and dinner in less than ten minutes," cried Birdie, rushing off. Ted mumbled something unintelligible and was after her.

"Birdie! I want to talk to you."

"Say it quick then," said Birdie, over her shoulder. "The doors open in three minnits."

"I can't tell you how grateful I am. This is no place to talk to you. Will you let me walk home with you to-night after your work's done?"

"Will I?" said Birdie, turning to face him. "I will not. Th' swell mob has shook you, an' a good thing it is. You was travelin' with a bunch of racers, when you was only built for medium speed. Now you're got your chance to a fresh start and don't you ever think I'm going to be the one to let you spoil it by beginnin' to walk out with a dinin'-room Lizzie like me."

"Don't say that, Birdie," Ted put in.

"It's the truth," affirmed Birdie. "Not that I ain't a perfec'ly respectable girrul, and ye know it. I'm a good slob, but folks would be tickled for the chance to say that you had nobody to go with but the likes av me. If I was to let you walk home with me to-night, yuh might be askin' to call next week. Inside half a year, if yuh was lonesome enough, yuh'd ask me to marry yuh. And b'gorra," she said softly, looking down at her unlovely red hands, "I'm dead scared I'd do it. Get back to work, Ted Terrill, and hold yer head up high, and when yuh say your prayers to-night, thank your lucky stars I ain't a hussy."

III

What She Wore

Somewhere in your story you must pause to describe your heroine's costume. It is a ticklish task. The average reader likes his heroine well dressed. He is not satisfied with knowing that she looked like a tall, fair lily. He wants to be told that her gown was of green crepe, with lace ruffles that swirled at her feet. Writers used to go so far as to name the dressmaker; and it was a poor kind of a heroine who didn't wear a red velvet by Worth. But that has been largely abandoned in these days of commissions. Still, when the heroine goes out on the terrace to spoon after dinner (a quaint old English custom for the origin of which see any novel by the "Duchess," page 179) the average reader wants to know what sort of a filmy wrap she snatches up on the way out. He demands a description, with as many illustrations as the publisher will stand for, of what she wore from the bedroom to the street, with full stops for the ribbons on her robe de nuit, and the buckles on her ballroom slippers. Half the poor creatures one sees flattening their noses against the shop windows are authors getting a line on the advance fashions. Suppose a careless writer were to dress his heroine in a full-plaited skirt only to find, when his story is published four months later, that full-plaited skirts have been relegated to the dim past!

I started to read a story once. It was a good one. There was in it not a single allusion to brandy-and-soda, or divorce, or the stock market. The dialogue crackled. The hero talked like a live man. It was a shipboard story, and the heroine was charming so long as she wore her heavy ulster. But along toward evening she blossomed forth in a yellow gown, with a scarlet poinsettia at her throat. I quit her cold. Nobody ever wore a scarlet poinsettia; or if they did, they couldn't wear it on a yellow gown. Or if they did wear it with a yellow gown, they didn't wear it at the throat. Scarlet poinsettias aren't worn, anyhow. To this day I don't know whether the heroine married the hero or jumped overboard.

You see, one can't be too careful about clothing one's heroine.

I hesitate to describe Sophy Epstein's dress. You won't like it. In the first place, it was cut too low, front and back, for a shoe clerk in a downtown loft. It was a black dress, near-princess in style, very tight as to fit, very short as to skirt, very sleazy as to material. It showed all the delicate curves of Sophy's under-fed, girlish body, and Sophy didn't care a bit. Its most objectionable feature was at the throat. Collarless gowns were in vogue. Sophy's daring shears had gone a snip or two farther. They had cut a startlingly generous V. To say that the dress was elbow-sleeved is superfluous. I have said that Sophy clerked in a downtown loft.

Sophy sold "sample" shoes at two-fifty a pair, and from where you were standing you thought they looked just like the shoes that were sold in the regular shops for six. When Sophy sat on one of the low benches at the feet of some customer, tugging away at a refractory shoe for a would-be small foot, her shameless little gown exposed more than it should have. But few of Sophy's customers were shocked. They were mainly chorus girls and ladies of doubtful complexion in search of cheap and ultra footgear, and—to use a health term—hardened by exposure.

Have I told you how pretty she was? She was so pretty that you immediately forgave her the indecency of her pitiful little gown. She was pretty in a daringly demure fashion, like a wicked little Puritan, or a poverty-stricken Cleo de Merode, with her smooth brown hair parted in the middle, drawn severely down over her ears, framing the lovely oval of her face and ending in a simple coil at the neck. Some serpent's wisdom had told Sophy to eschew puffs. But I think her prettiness could have triumphed even over those.

If Sophy's boss had been any other sort of man he would have informed Sophy, sternly, that black princess effects, cut low, were not au fait in the shoe-clerk world. But Sophy's boss had a rhombic nose, and no instep, and the tail of his name had been amputated. He didn't care how Sophy wore her dresses so long as she sold shoes.

Once the boss had kissed Sophy—not on the mouth, but just where her shabby gown formed its charming but immodest V. Sophy had slapped him, of course. But the slap had not set the thing right in her mind. She could not forget it. It had made her uncomfortable in much the same way as we are wildly ill at ease when we dream of walking naked in a crowded street. At odd moments during the day Sophy had found herself rubbing the spot furiously with her unlovely handkerchief, and shivering a little. She had never told the other girls about that kiss.

So—there you have Sophy and her costume. You may take her or leave her. I purposely placed these defects in costuming right at the beginning of the story, so that there should be no false pretenses. One more detail. About Sophy's throat was a slender, near-gold chain from which was suspended a cheap and glittering La Valliere. Sophy had not intended it as a sop to the conventions. It was an offering on the shrine of Fashion, and represented many lunchless days.

At eleven o'clock one August morning, Louie came to Chicago from Oskaloosa, Iowa. There was no hay in his hair. The comic papers have long insisted that the country boy, on his first visit to the city, is known by his greased boots and his high-water pants. Don't you believe them. The small-town boy is as fastidious about the height of his heels and the stripe of his shift and the roll of his hat-brim as are his city brothers. He peruses the slangily worded ads of the "classy clothes" tailors, and when scarlet cravats are worn the small-town boy is not more than two weeks late in acquiring one that glows like a headlight.

Louie found a rooming-house, shoved his suitcase under the bed, changed his collar, washed his hands in the gritty water of the wash bowl, and started out to look for a job.

Louie was twenty-one. For the last four years he had been employed in the best shoe store at home, and he knew shoe leather from the factory to the ash barrel. It was almost a religion with him.

Curiosity, which plays leads in so many life dramas, led Louie to the rotunda of the tallest building. It was built on the hollow center plan, with a sheer drop from the twenty-somethingth to the main floor. Louie stationed himself in the center of the mosaic floor, took off his hat, bent backward almost double and gazed, his mouth wide open. When he brought his muscles slowly back into normal position he tried hard not to look impressed. He glanced about, sheepishly, to see if any one was laughing at him, and his eye encountered the electric-lighted glass display case of the shoe company upstairs. The case was filled with pink satin slippers and cunning velvet boots, and the newest thing in bronze street shoes. Louie took the next elevator up. The shoe display had made him feel as though some one from home had slapped him on the back.

The God of the Jobless was with him. The boss had fired two boys the day before.

"Oskaloosa!" grinned the boss, derisively. "Do they wear shoes there? What do you know about shoes, huh, boy?"

Louie told him. The boss shuffled the papers on his desk, and chewed his cigar, and tried not to show his surprise. Louie, quite innocently, was teaching the boss things about the shoe business.

When Louie had finished—"Well, I try you, anyhow," the boss grunted, grudgingly. "I give you so-and-so much." He named a wage that would have been ridiculous if it had not been so pathetic.

"All right, sir," answered Louie, promptly, like the boys in the Alger series. The cost of living problem had never bothered Louie in Oskaloosa.

The boss hid a pleased smile.

"Miss Epstein!" he bellowed, "step this way! Miss Epstein, kindly show this here young man so he gets a line on the stock. He is from Oskaloosa, Ioway. Look out she don't sell you a gold brick, Louie."

But Louie was not listening. He was gazing at the V in Sophy Epstein's dress with all his scandalized Oskaloosa, Iowa, eyes.

Louie was no mollycoddle. But he had been in great demand as usher at the Young Men's Sunday Evening Club service at the Congregational church, and in his town there had been no Sophy Epsteins in too-tight princess dresses, cut into a careless V. But Sophy was a city product—I was about to say pure and simple, but I will not—wise, bold, young, old, underfed, overworked, and triumphantly pretty.

"How-do!" cooed Sophy in her best baby tones. Louie's disapproving eyes jumped from the objectionable V in Sophy's dress to the lure of Sophy's face, and their expression underwent a lightning change. There was no disapproving Sophy's face, no matter how long one had dwelt in Oskaloosa.

"I won't bite you," said Sophy. "I'm never vicious on Tuesdays. We'll start here with the misses' an' children's, and work over to the other side."

Whereupon Louie was introduced into the intricacies of the sample shoe business. He kept his eyes resolutely away from the V, and learned many things. He learned how shoes that look like six dollar values may be sold for two-fifty. He looked on in wide-eyed horror while Sophy fitted a No. 5 C shoe on a 6 B foot and assured the wearer that it looked like a made-to-order boot. He picked up a pair of dull kid shoes and looked at them. His leather-wise eyes saw much, and I think he would have taken his hat off the hook, and his offended business principles out of the shop forever if Sophy had not completed her purchase and strolled over to him at the psychological moment.

She smiled up at him, impudently. "Well, Pink Cheeks," she said, "how do you like our little settlement by the lake, huh?"

"These shoes aren't worth two-fifty," said Louie, indignation in his voice.

"Well, sure," replied Sophy. "I know it. What do you think this is? A charity bazaar?"

"But back home—" began Louie, hotly.

"Ferget it, kid," said Sophy. "This is a big town, but it ain't got no room for back-homers. Don't sour on one job till you've got another nailed. You'll find yourself cuddling down on a park bench if you do. Say, are you honestly from Oskaloosa?"

"I certainly am," answered Louie, with pride.

"My goodness!" ejaculated Sophy. "I never believed there was no such place. Don't brag about it to the other fellows."

"What time do you go out for lunch?" asked Louie.

"What's it to you?" with the accent on the "to."

"When I want to know a thing, I generally ask," explained Louie, gently.

Sophy looked at him—a long, keen, knowing look. "You'll learn," she observed, thoughtfully.

Louie did learn. He learned so much in that first week that when Sunday came it seemed as though aeons had passed over his head. He learned that the crime of murder was as nothing compared to the crime of allowing a customer to depart shoeless; he learned that the lunch hour was invented for the purpose of making dates; that no one had ever heard of Oskaloosa, Iowa; that seven dollars a week does not leave much margin for laundry and general recklessness; that a madonna face above a V-cut gown is apt to distract one's attention from shoes; that a hundred-dollar nest egg is as effective in Chicago as a pine stick would be in propping up a stone wall; and that all the other men clerks called Sophy "sweetheart."

Some of his newly acquired knowledge brought pain, as knowledge is apt to do.

He saw that State Street was crowded with Sophys during the noon hour; girls with lovely faces under pitifully absurd hats. Girls who aped the fashions of the dazzling creatures they saw stepping from limousines. Girls who starved body and soul in order to possess a set of false curls, or a pair of black satin shoes with mother-o'-pearl buttons. Girls whose minds were bounded on the north by the nickel theatres; on the east by

35

"I sez to him"; on the south by the gorgeous shop windows; and on the west by "He sez t' me."

Oh, I can't tell you how much Louie learned in that first week while his eyes were getting accustomed to the shifting, jostling, pushing, giggling, walking, talking throng. The city is justly famed as a hot house of forced knowledge.

One thing Louie could not learn. He could not bring himself to accept the V in Sophy's dress. Louie's mother had been one of the old-fashioned kind who wore a blue-and-white checked gingham apron from 6 A.M. to 2 P.M., when she took it off to go downtown and help the ladies of the church at the cake sale in the empty window of the gas company's office, only to don it again when she fried the potatoes for supper. Among other things she had taught Louie to wipe his feet before coming in, to respect and help women, and to change his socks often.

After a month of Chicago Louie forgot the first lesson; had more difficulty than I can tell you in reverencing a woman who only said, "Aw, don't get fresh now!" when the other men put their arms about her; and adhered to the third only after a struggle, in which he had to do a small private washing in his own wash-bowl in the evening.

Sophy called him a stiff. His gravely courteous treatment of her made her vaguely uncomfortable. She was past mistress in the art of parrying insults and banter, but she had no reply ready for Louie's boyish air of deference. It angered her for some unreasonable woman-reason.

There came a day when the V-cut dress brought them to open battle. I think Sophy had appeared that morning minus the chain and La Valliere. Frail and cheap as it was, it had been the only barrier that separated Sophy from frank shamelessness. Louie's outraged sense of propriety asserted itself.

"Sophy," he stammered, during a quiet half-hour, "I'll call for you and take you to the nickel show to-night if you'll promise not to wear that dress. What makes you wear that kind of a get-up, anyway?"

"Dress?" queried Sophy, looking down at the shiny front breadth of her frock. "Why? Don't you like it?"

"Like it! No!" blurted Louie.

"Don't yuh, rully! Deah me! Deah me! If I'd only knew that this morning. As a gen'ral thing I wear white duck complete down t' work, but I'm savin' my last two clean suits f'r gawlf."

Louie ran an uncomfortable finger around the edge of his collar, but he stood his ground. "It—it—shows your—neck so," he objected, miserably.

Sophy opened her great eyes wide. "Well, supposin' it does?" she inquired, coolly. "It's a perfectly good neck, ain't it?"

Louie, his face very red, took the plunge. "I don't know. I guess so. But, Sophy, it—looks so—so—you know what I mean. I hate to see the way the fellows rubber at you. Why don't you wear those plain shirt-waist things, with high collars, like my mother wears back home?"

Sophy's teeth came together with a click. She laughed a short cruel little laugh. "Say, Pink Cheeks, did yuh ever do a washin' from seven to twelve, after you got home from work in the evenin'? It's great! 'Specially when you're living in a six-by-ten room with all the modern inconveniences, includin' no water except on the third floor down. Simple! Say, a child could work it. All you got to do, when you get home so tired your back teeth ache, is to haul your water, an' soak your clothes, an' then rub 'em till your hands peel, and rinse 'em, an' boil 'em, and blue 'em, an' starch 'em. See? Just like that. Nothin' to it, kid. Nothin' to it."

Louie had been twisting his fingers nervously. Now his hands shut themselves into fists. He looked straight into Sophy's angry eyes.

"I do know what it is," he said, quite simply. "There's been a lot written and said about women's struggle with clothes. I wonder why they've never said anything about the way a man has to fight to keep up the thing they call appearances. God knows it's pathetic enough to think of a girl like you bending over a tubful of clothes. But when a man has to do it, it's a tragedy."

"That's so," agreed Sophy. "When a girl gets shabby, and her clothes begin t' look tacky she can take a gore or so out of her skirt where it's the most wore, and catch it in at the bottom, and call it a hobble. An' when her waist gets too soiled she can cover up the front of it with a jabot, an' if her face is pretty enough she can carry it off that way. But when a man is seedy, he's seedy. He can't sew no ruffles on his pants."

"I ran short last week," continued Louie. "That is, shorter than usual. I hadn't the fifty cents to give to the woman. You ought to see her! A little, gray-faced thing, with wisps of hair, and no chest to speak of, and one of those mashed-looking black hats. Nobody could have the nerve to ask her to wait for her money. So I did my own washing. I haven't learned to wear soiled clothes yet. I laughed fit to bust while I was doing it. But—I'll bet my mother dreamed of me that night. The way they do, you know, when something's gone wrong."

Sophy, perched on the third rung of the sliding ladder, was gazing at him. Her lips were parted slightly, and her cheeks were very pink. On her face was a new, strange look, as of something half forgotten. It was as though the spirit of Sophy-as-she-might-have-been were inhabiting her soul for a brief moment. At Louie's next words the look was gone.

"Can't you sew something—a lace yoke—or whatever you call 'em— in that dress?" he persisted.

"Aw, fade!" jeered Sophy. "When a girl's only got one dress it's got to have some tong to it. Maybe this gown would cause a wave of indignation in Oskaloosa, Iowa, but it don't even make a ripple on State Street. It takes more than an aggravated Dutch neck to make a fellow look at a girl these days. In a town like this a girl's got to make a showin' some way. I'm my own stage manager. They look at my dress first, an' grin. See? An' then they look at my face. I'm like the girl in the story. Muh face is muh fortune. It's earned me many a square meal; an' lemme tell you, Pink Cheeks, eatin' square meals is one of my favorite pastimes."

"Say, looka here!" bellowed the boss, wrathfully. "Just cut out this here Romeo and Juliet act, will you! That there ladder ain't for no balcony scene, understand. Here you, Louie, you shinny up there and get down a pair of them brown satin pumps, small size."

Sophy continued to wear the black dress. The V-cut neck seemed more flaunting than ever.

It was two weeks later that Louie came in from lunch, his face radiant. He was fifteen minutes late, but he listened to the boss's ravings with a smile.

"You grin like somebody handed you a ten-case note," commented Sophy, with a woman's curiosity. "I guess you must of met some rube from home when you was out t' lunch."

"Better than that! Who do you think I bumped right into in the elevator going down?"

"Well, Brothah Bones," mimicked Sophy, who did you meet in the elevator going down?"

"I met a man named Ames. He used to travel for a big Boston shoe house, and he made our town every few months. We got to be good friends. I took him home for Sunday dinner once, and he said it was the best dinner he'd had in months. You know how tired those traveling men get of hotel grub."

"Cut out the description and get down to action," snapped Sophy.

"Well, he knew me right away. And he made me go out to lunch with him. A real lunch, starting with soup. Gee! It went big. He asked me what I was doing. I told him I was working here, and he opened his eyes, and then he laughed and said: "How did you get into that joint?" Then he took me down to a swell little shoe shop on State Street, and it turned out that he owns it. He introduced me all around, and I'm going there to work next week. And wages! Why say, it's almost a salary. A fellow can hold his head up in a place like that."

"When you leavin'?" asked Sophy, slowly.

"Monday. Gee! it seems a year away."

Sophy was late Saturday morning. When she came in, hurriedly, her cheeks were scarlet and her eyes glowed. She took off her hat and coat and fell to straightening boxes and putting out stock without looking up. She took no part in the talk and jest that was going on among the other clerks. One of the men, in search of the missing mate to the shoe in his hand, came over to her, greeting her carelessly. Then he stared.

"Well, what do you know about this!" he called out to the others, and laughed coarsely, "Look, stop, listen! Little Sophy Bright Eyes here has pulled down the shades."

Louie turned quickly. The immodest V of Sophy's gown was filled with a black lace yoke that came up to the very lobes of her little pink ears. She had got some scraps of lace from—Where do they get those bits of rusty black? From some basement bargain counter, perhaps, raked over during the lunch hour. There were nine pieces in the front, and seven in the back. She had sat up half the night putting them together so that when completed they looked like one, if you didn't come too close. There is a certain strain of Indian patience and ingenuity in women that no man has ever been able to understand.

Louie looked up and saw. His eyes met Sophy's. In his there crept a certain exultant gleam, as of one who had fought for something great and won. Sophy saw the look. The shy questioning in her eyes was replaced by a spark of defiance. She tossed her head, and turned to the man who had called attention to her costume.

"Who's loony now?" she jeered. "I always put in a yoke when it gets along toward fall. My lungs is delicate. And anyway, I see by the papers yesterday that collarless gowns is slightly passay f'r winter."

IV

A Bush League Hero

This is not a baseball story. The grandstand does not rise as one man and shout itself hoarse with joy. There isn't a three-bagger in the entire three thousand words, and nobody is carried home on the shoulders of the crowd. For that sort of thing you need not squander fifteen cents on your favorite magazine. The modest sum of one cent will make you the possessor of a Pink 'Un. There you will find the season's games handled in masterly fashion by a six-best-seller artist, an expert mathematician, and an original-slang humorist. No mere short story dub may hope to compete with these.

In the old days, before the gentry of the ring had learned the wisdom of investing their winnings in solids instead of liquids, this used to be a favorite conundrum: When is a prize-fighter not a prize-fighter?

Chorus: When he is tending bar.

I rise to ask you Brothah Fan, when is a ball player not a ball player? Above the storm of facetious replies I shout the answer:

When he's a shoe clerk.

Any man who can look handsome in a dirty baseball suit is an Adonis. There is something about the baggy pants, and the Micawber-shaped collar, and the skull-fitting cap, and the foot or so of tan, or blue, or pink undershirt sleeve sticking out at the arms, that just naturally kills a man's best points. Then too, a baseball suit requires so much in the matter of leg. Therefore, when I say that Rudie Schlachweiler was a dream even in his baseball uniform, with a dirty brown streak right up the side of his pants where he had slid for base, you may know that the girls camped on the grounds during the season.

During the summer months our ball park is to us what the Grand Prix is to Paris, or Ascot is to London. What care we that Evers gets seven thousand a year (or is it a month?); or that Chicago's new South-side ball park seats thirty-five thousand (or is it million?). Of what interest are such meager items compared with the knowledge that

"Pug" Coulan, who plays short, goes with Undine Meyers, the girl up there in the eighth row, with the pink dress and the red roses on her hat? When "Pug" snatches a high one out of the firmament we yell with delight, and even as we yell we turn sideways to look up and see how Undine is taking it. Undine's shining eyes are fixed on "Pug," and he knows it, stoops to brush the dust off his dirt-begrimed baseball pants, takes an attitude of careless grace and misses the next play.

Our grandstand seats almost two thousand, counting the boxes. But only the snobs, and the girls with new hats, sit in the boxes. Box seats are comfortable, it is true, and they cost only an additional ten cents, but we have come to consider them undemocratic, and unworthy of true fans. Mrs. Freddy Van Dyne, who spends her winters in Egypt and her summers at the ball park, comes out to the game every afternoon in her automobile, but she never occupies a box seat; so why should we? She perches up in the grandstand with the rest of the enthusiasts, and when Kelly puts one over she stands up and clinches her fists, and waves her arms and shouts with the best of 'em. She has even been known to cry, "Good eye! Good eye!" when things were at fever heat. The only really blase individual in the ball park is Willie Grimes, who peddles ice-cream cones. For that matter, I once saw Willie turn a languid head to pipe, in his thin voice, "Give 'em a dark one, Dutch! Give 'em a dark one!"

Well, that will do for the firsh dash of local color. Now for the story.

Ivy Keller came home June nineteenth from Miss Shont's select school for young ladies. By June twenty-first she was bored limp. You could hardly see the plaits of her white tailored shirtwaist for fraternity pins and secret society emblems, and her bedroom was ablaze with college banners and pennants to such an extent that the maid gave notice every Thursday—which was upstairs cleaning day.

For two weeks after her return Ivy spent most of her time writing letters and waiting for them, and reading the classics on the front porch, dressed in a middy blouse and a blue skirt, with her hair done in a curly Greek effect like the girls on the covers of the *Ladies' Magazine*. She posed against the canvas bosom of the porch chair with one foot under her, the other swinging free, showing a tempting thing in beaded slipper, silk stocking, and what the story writers call "slim ankle."

On the second Saturday after her return her father came home for dinner at noon, found her deep in Volume Two of "Les Miserables."

"Whew! This is a scorcher!" he exclaimed, and dropped down on a wicker chair next to Ivy. Ivy looked at her father with languid interest, and smiled a daughterly smile. Ivy's father was an insurance man, alderman of his ward, president of the Civic Improvement Club, member of five lodges, and an habitual delegate. It generally was he who introduced distinguished guests who spoke at the opera house on Decoration Day. He called Mrs. Keller "Mother," and he wasn't above noticing the fit of a gown on a pretty feminine figure. He thought Ivy was an expurgated edition of Lillian Russell, Madame de Stael, and Mrs. Pankhurst.

"Aren't you feeling well, Ivy?" he asked. "Looking a little pale. It's the heat, I suppose. Gosh! Something smells good. Run in and tell Mother I'm here."

Ivy kept one slender finger between the leaves of her book. "I'm perfectly well," she replied. "That must be beefsteak and onions. Ugh!" And she shuddered, and went indoors.

Dad Keller looked after her thoughtfully. Then he went in, washed his hands, and sat down at table with Ivy and her mother.

"Just a sliver for me," said Ivy, "and no onions."

Her father put down his knife and fork, cleared his throat, and spake, thus:

"You get on your hat and meet me at the 2:45 inter-urban. You're going to the ball game with me."

"Ball game!" repeated Ivy. "I? But I'd—"

"Yes, you do," interrupted her father. "You've been moping around here looking a cross between Saint Cecilia and Little Eva long enough. I don't care if you don't know a spitball from a fadeaway when you see it. You'll be out in the air all afternoon, and there'll be some excitement. All the girls go. You'll like it. They're playing Marshalltown."

Ivy went, looking the sacrificial lamb. Five minutes after the game was called she pointed one tapering white finger in the direction of the pitcher's mound.

"Who's that?" she asked.

"Pitcher," explained Papa Keller, laconically. Then, patiently: "He throws the ball."

"Oh," said Ivy. "What did you say his name was?"

"I didn't say. But it's Rudie Schlachweiler. The boys call him Dutch. Kind of a pet, Dutch is."

"Rudie Schlachweiler!" murmured Ivy, dreamily. "What a strong name!"

"Want some peanuts?" inquired her father.

"Does one eat peanuts at a ball game?"

"It ain't hardly legal if you don't," Pa Keller assured her.

"Two sacks," said Ivy. "Papa, why do they call it a diamond, and what are those brown bags at the corners, and what does it count if you hit the ball, and why do they rub their hands in the dust and then—er—spit on them, and what salary does a pitcher get, and why does the red-haired man on the other side dance around like that between the second and third brown bag, and doesn't a pitcher do anything but pitch, and wh—?"

"You're on," said papa.

After that Ivy didn't miss a game during all the time that the team played in the home town. She went without a new hat, and didn't care whether Jean Valjean got away with the goods or not, and forgot whether you played third hand high or low in bridge. She even became chummy with Undine Meyers, who wasn't her kind of a girl at all. Undine was thin in a voluptuous kind of way, if such a paradox can be, and she had red lips, and a roving eye, and she ran around downtown without a hat more than was strictly necessary. But Undine and Ivy had two subjects in common. They were baseball and love. It is queer how the limelight will make heroes of us all.

Now "Pug" Coulan, who was red-haired, and had shoulders like an ox, and arms that hung down to his knees, like those of an orang-outang, slaughtered beeves at the Chicago stockyards in winter. In the summer he slaughtered hearts. He wore mustard colored shirts that matched his hair, and his baseball stockings generally had a rip in them somewhere, but when he was on the diamond we were almost ashamed to look at Undine, so wholly did her heart shine in her eyes.

Now, we'll have just another dash or two of local color. In a small town the chances for hero worship are few. If it weren't for the traveling men our girls wouldn't know whether stripes or checks were the thing in gents' suitings. When the baseball season opened the girls swarmed on it. Those that didn't understand baseball pretended they did. When the team was out of town our form of greeting was changed from, "Good-morning!" or "Howdy-do!" to "What's the score?" Every night the results of the games throughout the league were posted up on the blackboard in front of Schlager's hardware store, and to see the way in which the crowd stood around it, and streamed across the street toward it, you'd have thought they were giving away gas stoves and hammock couches.

Going home in the street car after the game the girls used to gaze adoringly at the dirty faces of their sweat-begrimed heroes, and then they'd rush home, have supper, change their dresses, do their hair, and rush downtown past the Parker Hotel to mail their letters. The baseball boys boarded over at the Griggs House, which is third-class, but they used their tooth-picks, and held the postmortem of the day's game out in front of the Parker Hotel, which is our leading hostelry. The post-office receipts record for our town was broken during the months of June, July, and August.

Mrs. Freddy Van Dyne started the trouble by having the team over to dinner, "Pug" Coulan and all. After all, why not? No foreign and impecunious princes penetrate as far inland as our town. They get only as far as New York, or Newport, where they are gobbled up by many-moneyed matrons. If Mrs. Freddy Van Dyne found the supply of available lions limited, why should she not try to content herself with a jackal or so?

Ivy was asked. Until then she had contented herself with gazing at her hero. She had become such a hardened baseball fan that she followed the game with a score card, accurately jotting down every play, and keeping her watch open on her knee.

She sat next to Rudie at dinner. Before she had nibbled her second salted almond, Ivy Keller and Rudie Schlachweiler understood each other. Rudie illustrated certain plays by drawing lines on the table-cloth with his knife and Ivy gazed, wide-eyed, and allowed her soup to grow cold.

The first night that Rudie called, Pa Keller thought it a great joke. He sat out on the porch with Rudie and Ivy and talked baseball, and got up to show Rudie how he could have got the goat of that Keokuk catcher if only he had tried one of his famous open-faced throws. Rudie looked politely interested, and laughed in all the right places. But Ivy didn't need to pretend. Rudie Schlachweiler spelled baseball to her. She did not think of her caller as a good-looking young man in a blue serge suit and a white shirtwaist. Even as he sat there she saw him as a blonde god standing on the pitcher's mound, with the scars of battle on his baseball pants, his left foot placed in front of him at right angles with his right foot, his gaze fixed on first base in a cunning effort to deceive the man at bat, in that favorite attitude of pitchers just before they get ready to swing their left leg and h'ist one over.

44

The second time that Rudie called, Ma Keller said:

"Ivy, I don't like that ball player coming here to see you. The neighbors'll talk."

The third time Rudie called, Pa Keller said: "What's that guy doing here again?"

The fourth time Rudie called, Pa Keller and Ma Keller said, in unison: "This thing has got to stop."

But it didn't. It had had too good a start. For the rest of the season Ivy met her knight of the sphere around the corner. Theirs was a walking courtship. They used to roam up as far as the State road, and down as far as the river, and Rudie would fain have talked of love, but Ivy talked of baseball.

"Darling," Rudie would murmur, pressing Ivy's arm closer, "when did you first begin to care?"

"Why I liked the very first game I saw when Dad—"

"I mean, when did you first begin to care for me?"

"Oh! When you put three men out in that game with Marshalltown when the teams were tied in the eighth inning. Remember? Say, Rudie dear, what was the matter with your arm to-day? You let three men walk, and Albia's weakest hitter got a home run out of you."

"Oh, forget baseball for a minute, Ivy! Let's talk about something else. Let's talk about—us."

"Us? Well, you're baseball, aren't you?" retorted Ivy. "And if you are, I am. Did you notice the way that Ottumwa man pitched yesterday? He didn't do any acting for the grandstand. He didn't reach up above his head, and wrap his right shoulder with his left toe, and swing his arm three times and then throw seven inches outside the plate. He just took the ball in his hand, looked at it curiously for a moment, and fired it—zing!—like that, over the plate. I'd get that ball if I were you."

"Isn't this a grand night?" murmured Rudie.

"But they didn't have a hitter in the bunch," went on Ivy. "And not a man in the team could run. That's why they're tail-enders. Just the same, that man on the mound was a wizard, and if he had one decent player to give him some support—"

Well, the thing came to a climax. One evening, two weeks before the close of the season, Ivy put on her hat and announced that she was going downtown to mail her letters.

"Mail your letters in the daytime," growled Papa Keller.

"I didn't have time to-day," answered Ivy. "It was a thirteen inning game, and it lasted until six o'clock."

It was then that Papa Keller banged the heavy fist of decision down on the library table.

"This thing's got to stop!" he thundered. "I won't have any girl of mine running the streets with a ball player, understand? Now you quit seeing this seventy-five-dollars-a-month bush leaguer or leave this house. I mean it."

"All right," said Ivy, with a white-hot calm. "I'll leave. I can make the grandest kind of angel-food with marshmallow icing, and you know yourself my fudges can't be equaled. He'll be playing in the major leagues in three years. Why just yesterday there was a strange man at the game—a city man, you could tell by his hat-band, and the way his clothes were cut. He stayed through the whole game, and never took his eyes off Rudie. I just know he was a scout for the Cubs."

"Probably a hardware drummer, or a fellow that Schlachweiler owes money to."

Ivy began to pin on her hat. A scared look leaped into Papa Keller's eyes. He looked a little old, too, and drawn, at that minute. He stretched forth a rather tremulous hand.

"Ivy-girl," he said.

"What?" snapped Ivy.

"Your old father's just talking for your own good. You're breaking your ma's heart. You and me have been good pals, haven't we?"

"Yes," said Ivy, grudgingly, and without looking up.

"Well now, look here. I've got a proposition to make to you. The season's over in two more weeks. The last week they play out of town. Then the boys'll come back for a week or so, just to hang around town and try to get used to the idea of leaving us. Then they'll scatter to take up their winter jobs—cutting ice, most of 'em," he added, grimly.

"Mr. Schlachweiler is employed in a large establishment in Slatersville, Ohio," said Ivy, with dignity. "He regards baseball as his profession, and he cannot do anything that would affect his pitching arm."

Pa Keller put on the tremolo stop and brought a misty look into his eyes.

"Ivy, you'll do one last thing for your old father, won't you?"

"Maybe," answered Ivy, coolly.

"Don't make that fellow any promises. Now wait a minute! Let me get through. I won't put any crimp in your plans. I won't speak to

Schlachweiler. Promise you won't do anything rash until the ball season's over. Then we'll wait just one month, see? Till along about November. Then if you feel like you want to see him—"

"But how—"

"Hold on. You mustn't write to him, or see him, or let him write to you during that time, see? Then, if you feel the way you do now, I'll take you to Slatersville to see him. Now that's fair, ain't it? Only don't let him know you're coming."

" M-m-m-yes," said Ivy.

"Shake hands on it." She did. Then she left the room with a rush, headed in the direction of her own bedroom. Pa Keller treated himself to a prodigious wink and went out to the vegetable garden in search of Mother.

The team went out on the road, lost five games, won two, and came home in fourth place. For a week they lounged around the Parker Hotel and held up the street corners downtown, took many farewell drinks, then, slowly, by ones and twos, they left for the packing houses, freight depots, and gents' furnishing stores from whence they came.

October came in with a blaze of sumac and oak leaves. Ivy stayed home and learned to make veal loaf and apple pies. The worry lines around Pa Keller's face began to deepen. Ivy said that she didn't believe that she cared to go back to Miss Shont's select school for young ladies.

October thirty-first came.

"We'll take the eight-fifteen to-morrow," said her father to Ivy.

"All right," said Ivy.

"Do you know where he works?" asked he.

"No," answered Ivy.

"That'll be all right. I took the trouble to look him up last August."

The short November afternoon was drawing to its close (as our best talent would put it) when Ivy and her father walked along the streets of Slatersville. (I can't tell you what streets, because I don't know.) Pa Keller brought up before a narrow little shoe shop.

"Here we are," he said, and ushered Ivy in. A short, stout, proprietary figure approached them smiling a mercantile smile.

"What can I do for you?" he inquired.

Ivy's eyes searched the shop for a tall, golden-haired form in a soiled baseball suit.

"We'd like to see a gentleman named Schlachweiler—Rudolph Schlachweiler," said Pa Keller.

47

"Anything very special?" inquired the proprietor. "He's—rather busy just now. Wouldn't anybody else do? Of course, if—"

"No," growled Keller.

The boss turned. "Hi! Schlachweiler!" he bawled toward the rear of the dim little shop.

"Yessir," answered a muffled voice.

"Front!" yelled the boss, and withdrew to a safe listening distance.

A vaguely troubled look lurked in the depths of Ivy's eyes. From behind the partition of the rear of the shop emerged a tall figure. It was none other than our hero. He was in his shirt- sleeves, and he struggled into his coat as he came forward, wiping his mouth with the back of his hand, hurriedly, and swallowing.

I have said that the shop was dim. Ivy and her father stood at one side, their backs to the light. Rudie came forward, rubbing his hands together in the manner of clerks.

"Something in shoes?" he politely inquired. Then he saw.

"Ivy!—ah—Miss Keller!" he exclaimed. Then, awkwardly: "Well, how-do, Mr. Keller. I certainly am glad to see you both. How's the old town? What are you doing in Slatersville?"

"Why—Ivy—" began Pa Keller, blunderingly.

But Ivy clutched his arm with a warning hand. The vaguely troubled look in her eyes had become wildly so.

"Schlachweiler!" shouted the voice of the boss. "Customers!" and he waved a hand in the direction of the fitting benches.

"All right, sir," answered Rudie. "Just a minute."

"Dad had to come on business," said Ivy, hurriedly. "And he brought me with him. I'm—I'm on my way to school in Cleveland, you know. Awfully glad to have seen you again. We must go. That lady wants her shoes, I'm sure, and your employer is glaring at us. Come, Dad."

At the door she turned just in time to see Rudie removing the shoe from the pudgy foot of the fat lady customer.

We'll take a jump of six months. That brings us into the lap of April.

Pa Keller looked up from his evening paper. Ivy, home for the Easter vacation, was at the piano. Ma Keller was sewing.

Pa Keller cleared his throat. "I see by the paper," he announced, "that Schlachweiler's been sold to Des Moines. Too bad we lost him. He was a great little pitcher, but he played in bad luck. Whenever he was on the slab the boys seemed to give him poor support."

"Fudge!" exclaimed Ivy, continuing to play, but turning a spirited face toward her father. "What piffle! Whenever a player pitches rotten ball you'll always hear him howling about the support he didn't get. Schlachweiler was a bum pitcher. Anybody could hit him with a willow wand, on a windy day, with the sun in his eyes."

V

The Kitchen Side of the Door

The City was celebrating New Year's Eve. Spelled thus, with a capital C, know it can mean but New York. In the Pink Fountain Room of the Newest Hotel all those grand old forms and customs handed down to us for the occasion were being rigidly observed in all their original quaintness. The Van Dyked man who looked like a Russian Grand Duke (he really was a chiropodist) had drunk champagne out of the pink satin slipper of the lady who behaved like an actress (she was forelady at Schmaus' Wholesale Millinery, eighth floor). The two respectable married ladies there in the corner had been kissed by each other's husbands. The slim, Puritan-faced woman in white, with her black hair so demurely parted and coiled in a sleek knot, had risen suddenly from her place and walked indolently to the edge of the plashing pink fountain in the center of the room, had stood contemplating its shallows with a dreamy half-smile on her lips, and then had lifted her slim legs slowly and gracefully over its fern-fringed basin and had waded into its chilling midst, trailing her exquisite white satin and chiffon draperies after her, and scaring the goldfish into fits. The loudest scream of approbation had come from the yellow-haired, loose-lipped youth who had made the wager, and lost it. The heavy blonde in the inevitable violet draperies showed signs of wanting to dance on the table. Her companion—a structure made up of layer upon layer, and fold upon fold of flabby tissue—knew all the waiters by their right names, and insisted on singing with the orchestra and beating time with a rye roll. The clatter of dishes was giving way to the clink of glasses.

In the big, bright kitchen back of the Pink Fountain Room Miss Gussie Fink sat at her desk, calm, watchful, insolent-eyed, a goddess sitting in judgment. On the pay roll of the Newest Hotel Miss Gussie Fink's name appeared as kitchen checker, but her regular job was goddessing. Her altar was a high desk in a corner of the busy kitchen, and it was an altar of incense, of burnt-offerings, and of showbread. Inexorable as a goddess of the ancients was Miss Fink, and ten times as difficult to appease. For this is the rule of the Newest Hotel, that no waiter may carry his laden tray restaurantward until its contents have been viewed and duly checked by the eye and hand of Miss Gussie Fink, or her assistants. Flat upon the table must go every tray, off must go each silver dish-cover, lifted must be each napkin to disclose its treasure of steaming corn or hot rolls. Clouds of incense rose before Miss Gussie Fink and she sniffed it unmoved, her eyes, beneath level brows, regarding savory broiler or cunning ice with equal indifference, appraising alike lobster cocktail or onion soup, traveling from blue points to brie. Things a la and things glace were all one to her. Gazing at food was Miss Gussie Fink's occupation, and just to see the way she regarded a boneless squab made you certain that she never ate.

In spite of the I-don't-know-how-many (see ads) New Year's Eve diners for whom food was provided that night, the big, busy kitchen was the most orderly, shining, spotless place imaginable. But Miss Gussie Fink was the neatest, most immaculate object in all that great, clean room. There was that about her which suggested daisies in a field, if you know what I mean. This may have been due to the fact that her eyes were brown while her hair was gold, or it may have been something about the way her collars fitted high, and tight, and smooth, or the way her close white sleeves came down to meet her pretty hands, or the way her shining hair sprang from her forehead. Also the smooth creaminess of her clear skin may have had something to do with it. But privately, I think it was due to the way she wore her shirtwaists. Miss Gussie Fink could wear a starched white shirtwaist under a close-fitting winter coat, remove the coat, run her right forefinger along her collar's edge and her left thumb along the back of her belt and disclose to the admiring world a blouse as unwrinkled and unsullied as though it had just come from her own skilful hands at the ironing board. Miss Gussie Fink was so innately, flagrantly, beautifully clean-looking that—well, there must be a stop to this description.

She was the kind of girl you'd like to see behind the counter of your favorite delicatessen, knowing that you need not shudder as her fingers touch your Sunday night supper slices of tongue, and Swiss cheese, and ham. No girl had ever dreamed of refusing to allow Gussie to borrow her chamois for a second.

To-night Miss Fink had come on at 10 P.M., which was just two hours later than usual. She knew that she was to work until 6 A.M., which may have accounted for the fact that she displayed very little of what the fans call ginger as she removed her hat and coat and hung them on the hook behind the desk. The prospect of that all-night, eight-hour stretch may have accounted for it, I say. But privately, and *entre nous,* it didn't. For here you must know of Heiny. Heiny, alas! now Henri.

Until two weeks ago Henri had been Heiny and Miss Fink had been Kid. When Henri had been Heiny he had worked in the kitchen at many things, but always with a loving eye on Miss Gussie Fink. Then one wild night there had been a waiters' strike—wages or hours or tips or all three. In the confusion that followed Heiny had been pressed into service and a chopped coat. He had fitted into both with unbelievable nicety, proving that waiters are born, not made. Those little tricks and foibles that are characteristic of the genus waiter seemed to envelop him as though a fairy garment had fallen upon his shoulders. The folded napkin under his left arm seemed to have been placed there by nature, so perfectly did it fit into place. The ghostly tread, the little whisking skip, the half-simper, the deferential bend that had in it at the same time something of insolence, all were there; the very "Yes, miss," and "Very good, sir," rose automatically and correctly to his untrained lips. Cinderella rising resplendent from her ash-strewn hearth was not more completely transformed than Heiny in his role of Henri. And with the transformation Miss Gussie Fink had been left behind her desk disconsolate.

Kitchens are as quick to seize upon these things and gossip about them as drawing rooms are. And because Miss Gussie Fink had always worn a little air of aloofness to all except Heiny, the kitchen was the more eager to make the most of its morsel. Each turned it over under his tongue—Tony, the Crook, whom Miss Fink had scorned; Francois, the entree cook, who often forgot he was married; Miss Sweeney, the bar-checker, who was jealous of Miss Fink's complexion. Miss Fink heard, and said nothing. She only knew that there would be no dear figure waiting for her when the night's work was done. For two weeks now she had put on her hat and coat and gone her way at one o'clock alone. She discovered that to be taken home night after night under Heiny's tender escort had taught her a ridiculous terror of the streets at night now that she was without protection. Always the short walk from the car to the flat where Miss Fink lived with her mother had been a glorious, star-lit, all too brief moment. Now it was an endless and terrifying trial, a thing of shivers and dread, fraught with horror of passing the alley just back of Cassidey's buffet. There had even been certain little half-serious, half-jesting talks about the future into which there had entered the subject of a little delicatessen and restaurant in a desirable neighborhood, with Heiny in the kitchen, and a certain blonde, neat, white-shirtwaisted person in charge of the desk and front shop.

She and her mother had always gone through a little formula upon Miss Fink's return from work. They never used it now. Gussie's mother was a real mother—the kind that wakes up when you come home.

"That you, Gussie?" Ma Fink would call from the bedroom, at the sound of the key in the lock.

"It's me, Ma."

"Heiny bring you home?"

"Sure," happily.

"There's a bit of sausage left, and some pie if—"

"Oh, I ain't hungry. We stopped at Joey's downtown and had a cup of coffee and a ham on rye. Did you remember to put out the milk bottle?"

For two weeks there had been none of that. Gussie had learned to creep silently into bed, and her mother, being a mother, feigned sleep.

To-night at her desk Miss Gussie Fink seemed a shade cooler, more self-contained, and daisylike than ever. From somewhere at the back of her head she could see that Heiny was avoiding her desk and was using the services of the checker at the other end of the room. And even as the poison of this was eating into her heart she was tapping her forefinger imperatively on the desk before her and saying to Tony, the Crook:

"Down on the table with that tray, Tony—flat. This may be a busy little New Year's Eve, but you can't come any of your sleight-of-hand stuff on me." For Tony had a little trick of concealing a dollar-and-a-quarter sirloin by the simple method of slapping the platter close to the underside of his tray and holding it there with long, lean fingers outspread, the entire bit of knavery being concealed in the folds of a flowing white napkin in the hand that balanced the tray. Into Tony's eyes there came a baleful gleam. His lean jaw jutted out threateningly.

"You're the real Weissenheimer kid, ain't you?" he sneered. "Never mind. I'll get you at recess."

"Some day," drawled Miss Fink, checking the steak, "the house'll get wise to your stuff and then you'll have to go back to the coal wagon. I know so much about you it's beginning to make me uncomfortable. I hate to carry around a burden of crime."

"You're a sorehead because Heiny turned you down and now—"

"Move on there!" snapped Miss Fink, "or I'll call the steward to settle you. Maybe he'd be interested to know that you've been counting in the date and your waiter's number, and adding 'em in at the bottom of your check."

Tony, the Crook, turned and skimmed away toward the dining-room, but the taste of victory was bitter in Miss Fink's mouth.

Midnight struck. There came from the direction of the Pink Fountain Room a clamor and din which penetrated the thickness of the padded doors that separated the dining-room from the kitchen beyond. The sound rose and swelled above the blare of the orchestra. Chairs scraped on the marble floor as hundreds rose to their feet. The sound of clinking glasses became as the jangling of a hundred bells. There came the sharp spat of hand-clapping, then cheers, yells, huzzas. Through the swinging doors at the end of the long passageway Miss Fink could catch glimpses of dazzling color, of shimmering gowns, of bare arms uplifted, of flowers, and plumes, and jewels, with the rosy light of the famed pink fountain casting a gracious glow over all. Once she saw a tall young fellow throw his arm about the shoulder of a glorious creature at the next table, and though the door swung shut before she could see it, Miss Fink knew that he had kissed her.

There were no New Year's greetings in the kitchen back of the Pink Fountain Room. It was the busiest moment in all that busy night. The heat of the ovens was so intense that it could be felt as far as Miss Fink's remote corner. The swinging doors between dining-room and kitchen were never still. A steady stream of waiters made for the steam tables before which the white-clad chefs stood ladling, carving, basting, serving, gave their orders, received them, stopped at the checking-desk, and sped dining-roomward again. Tony, the Crook, was cursing at one of the little Polish vegetable girls who had not been quick enough about the garnishing of a salad, and she was saying, over and over again, in her thick tongue:

"Aw, shod op yur mout'!"

The thud-thud of Miss Fink's checking-stamp kept time to flying footsteps, but even as her practised eye swept over the tray before her she saw the steward direct Henri toward her desk, just as he was about to head in the direction of the minor checking-desk. Beneath downcast lids she saw him coming. There was about Henri to-night a certain radiance, a sort of electrical elasticity, so nimble, so tireless, so exuberant was he. In the eyes of Miss Gussie Fink he looked heartbreakingly handsome in his waiter's uniform—handsome, distinguished, remote, and infinitely desirable. And just behind him, revenge in his eye, came Tony.

The flat surface of the desk received Henri's tray. Miss Fink regarded it with a cold and business-like stare. Henri whipped his napkin from under his left arm and began to remove covers, dexterously. Off came the first silver, dome-shaped top.

"Guinea hen," said Henri.

"I seen her lookin' at you when you served the little necks," came from Tony, as though continuing a conversation begun in some past moment of pause, "and she's some lovely doll, believe me."

Miss Fink scanned the guinea hen thoroughly, but with a detached air, and selected the proper stamp from the box at her elbow. Thump! On the broad pasteboard sheet before her appeared the figures $1.75 after Henri's number.

"Think so?" grinned Henri, and removed another cover. "One candied sweets."

"I bet some day we'll see you in the Sunday papers, Heiny," went on Tony, "with a piece about handsome waiter runnin' away with beautiful s'ciety girl. Say; you're too perfect even for a waiter."

Thump! Thirty cents.

"Quit your kiddin'," said the flattered Henri. "One endive, French dressing."

Thump! "Next!" said Miss Fink, dispassionately, yawned, and smiled fleetingly at the entree cook who wasn't looking her way. Then, as Tony slid his tray toward her: "How's business, Tony? H'm? How many two-bit cigar bands have you slipped onto your own private collection of nickel straights and made a twenty-cent rake-off?"

But there was a mist in the bright brown eyes as Tony, the Crook, turned away with his tray. In spite of the satisfaction of having had the last word, Miss Fink knew in her heart that Tony had "got her at recess," as he had said he would.

Things were slowing up for Miss Fink. The stream of hurrying waiters was turned in the direction of the kitchen bar now. From now on the eating would be light, and the drinking heavy. Miss Fink, with time hanging heavy, found herself blinking down at the figures stamped on the pasteboard sheet before her, and in spite of the blinking, two marks that never were intended for a checker's report splashed down just over the $1.75 after Henri's number. A lovely doll! And she had gazed at Heiny. Well, that was to be expected. No woman could gaze unmoved upon Heiny. "A lovely doll—"

"Hi, Miss Fink!" it was the steward's voice. "We need you over in the bar to help Miss Sweeney check the drinks. They're coming too swift for her. The eating will be light from now on; just a little something salty now and then."

So Miss Fink dabbed covertly at her eyes and betook herself out of the atmosphere of roasting, and broiling, and frying, and stewing; away from the sight of great copper kettles, and glowing coals and hissing pans, into a little world fragrant with mint, breathing of orange and lemon peel, perfumed with pineapple, redolent of cinnamon and clove, reeking with things spirituous. Here the splutter of the broiler was replaced by the hiss of the siphon, and the pop-pop of corks, and the tinkle and clink of ice against glass.

"Hello, dearie!" cooed Miss Sweeney, in greeting, staring hard at the suspicious redness around Miss Fink's eyelids. "Ain't you sweet to come over here in the headache department and help me out! Here's the wine list. You'll prob'ly need it. Say, who do you suppose invented New Year's Eve? They must of had a imagination like a Greek bus boy. I'm limp as a rag now, and it's only two-thirty. I've got a regular cramp in my wrist from checkin' quarts. Say, did you hear about Heiny's crowd?"

"No," said Miss Fink, evenly, and began to study the first page of the wine list under the heading "Champagnes of Noted Vintages."

"Well," went on Miss Sweeney's little thin, malicious voice, "he's fell in soft. There's a table of three, and they're drinkin' 1874 Imperial Crown at twelve dollars per, like it was Waukesha ale. And every time they finish a bottle one of the guys pays for it with a brand new ten and a brand new five and tells Heiny to keep the change. Can you beat it?"

"I hope," said Miss Fink, pleasantly, "that the supply of 1874 will hold out till morning. I'd hate to see them have to come down to ten dollar wine. Here you, Tony! Come back here! I may be a new hand in this department but I'm not so green that you can put a gold label over on me as a yellow label. Notice that I'm checking you another fifty cents."

"Ain't he the grafter!" laughed Miss Sweeney. She leaned toward Miss Fink and lowered her voice discreetly. "Though I'll say this for'm. If you let him get away with it now an' then, he'll split even with you. H'm? O, well, now, don't get so high and mighty. The management expects it in this department. That's why they pay starvation wages."

An unusual note of color crept into Miss Gussie Fink's smooth cheek. It deepened and glowed as Heiny darted around the corner and up to the bar. There was about him an air of suppressed excitement—suppressed, because Heiny was too perfect a waiter to display emotion.

"Not another!" chanted the bartenders, in chorus.

"Yes," answered Henri, solemnly, and waited while the wine cellar was made to relinquish another rare jewel.

"O, you Heiny!" called Miss Sweeney, "tell us what she looks like. If I had time I'd take a peek myself. From what Tony says she must look something like Maxine Elliot, only brighter."

Henri turned. He saw Miss Fink. A curious little expression came into his eyes—a Heiny look, it might have been called, as he regarded his erstwhile sweetheart's unruffled attire, and clear skin, and steady eye and glossy hair. She was looking past him in that baffling, maddening way that angry women have. Some of Henri's poise seemed to desert him in that moment. He appeared a shade less debonair as he received the precious bottle from the wine man's hands. He made for Miss Fink's desk and stood watching her while she checked his order. At the door he turned and looked over his shoulder at Miss Sweeney.

"Some time," he said, deliberately, "when there's no ladies around, I'll tell you what I think she looks like."

And the little glow of color in Miss Gussie Fink's smooth cheek became a crimson flood that swept from brow to throat.

"Oh, well," snickered Miss Sweeney, to hide her own discomfiture, "this is little Heiny's first New Year's Eve in the dining-room. Honest, I b'lieve he's shocked. He don't realize that celebratin' New Year's Eve is like eatin' oranges. You got to let go your dignity t' really enjoy 'em."

Three times more did Henri enter and demand a bottle of the famous vintage, and each time he seemed a shade less buoyant. His elation diminished as his tips grew greater until, as he drew up at the bar at six o'clock, he seemed wrapped in impenetrable gloom.

"Them hawgs sousin' yet?" shrilled Miss Sweeney. She and Miss Fink had climbed down from their high stools, and were preparing to leave. Henri nodded, drearily, and disappeared in the direction of the Pink Fountain Room.

Miss Fink walked back to her own desk in the corner near the dining-room door. She took her hat off the hook, and stood regarding it, thoughtfully. Then, with a little air of decision, she turned and walked swiftly down the passageway that separated dining-room from kitchen.

Tillie, the scrub-woman, was down on her hands and knees in one corner of the passage. She was one of a small army of cleaners that had begun the work of clearing away the debris of the long night's revel. Miss Fink lifted her neat skirts high as she tip-toed through the little soapy pool that followed in the wake of Tillie, the scrub-woman. She opened the swinging doors a cautious little crack and peered in. What she saw was not pretty. If the words sordid and bacchanalian had been part of Miss Fink's vocabulary they would have risen to her lips then. The crowd had gone. The great room contained not more than half a dozen people. Confetti littered the floor. Here and there a napkin, crushed and bedraggled into an unrecognizable ball, lay under a table. From an overturned bottle the dregs were dripping drearily. The air was stale, stifling, poisonous.

At a little table in the center of the room Henri's three were still drinking. They were doing it in a dreadful and businesslike way. There were two men and one woman. The faces of all three were mahogany colored and expressionless. There was about them an awful sort of stillness. Something in the sight seemed to sicken Gussie Fink. It came to her that the wintry air outdoors must be gloriously sweet, and cool, and clean in contrast to this. She was about to turn away, with a last look at Heiny yawning behind his hand, when suddenly the woman rose unsteadily to her feet, balancing herself with her finger tips on the table. She raised her head and stared across the room with dull, unseeing eyes, and licked her lips with her tongue. Then she turned and walked half a dozen paces, screamed once with horrible shrillness, and crashed to the floor. She lay there in a still, crumpled heap, the folds of her exquisite gown rippling to meet a little stale pool of wine that had splashed from some broken glass. Then this happened. Three people ran toward the woman on the floor, and two people ran past her and out of the room. The two who ran away were the men with whom she had been drinking, and they were not seen again. The three who ran toward her were Henri, the waiter, Miss Gussie Fink, checker, and Tillie, the scrub-woman. Henri and Miss Fink reached her first. Tillie, the scrub-woman, was a close third. Miss Gussie Fink made as though to slip her arm under the poor bruised head, but Henri caught her wrist fiercely (for a waiter) and pulled her to her feet almost roughly.

"You leave her alone, Kid," he commanded.

Miss Gussie Fink stared, indignation choking her utterance. And as she stared the fierce light in Henri's eyes was replaced by the light of tenderness.

"We'll tend to her," said Henri; "she ain't fit for you to touch. I wouldn't let you soil your hands on such truck." And while Gussie still stared he grasped the unconscious woman by the shoulders, while another waiter grasped her ankles, with Tillie, the scrub-woman, arranging her draperies pityingly around her, and together they carried her out of the dining-room to a room beyond.

Back in the kitchen Miss Gussie Fink was preparing to don her hat, but she was experiencing some difficulty because of the way in which her fingers persisted in trembling. Her face was turned away from the swinging doors, but she knew when Henri came in. He stood just behind her, in silence. When she turned to face him she found Henri looking at her, and as he looked all the Heiny in him came to the surface and shone in his eyes. He looked long and silently at Miss Gussie Fink—at the sane, simple, wholesomeness of her, at her clear brown eyes, at her white forehead from which the shining hair sprang away in such a delicate line, at her immaculately white shirtwaist, and her smooth, snug-fitting collar that came up to the lobes of her little pink ears, at her creamy skin, at her trim belt. He looked as one who would rest his eyes—eyes weary of gazing upon satins, and jewels, and rouge, and carmine, and white arms, and bosoms.

"Gee, Kid! You look good to me," he said.

"Do I—Heiny?" whispered Miss Fink.

"Believe me!" replied Heiny, fervently. "It was just a case of swelled head. Forget it, will you? Say, that gang in there to-night—why, say, that gang—"

"I know," interrupted Miss Fink.

"Going home?" asked Heiny.

"Yes."

"Suppose we have a bite of something to eat first," suggested Heiny.

Miss Fink glanced round the great, deserted kitchen. As she gazed a little expression of disgust wrinkled her pretty nose—the nose that perforce had sniffed the scent of so many rare and exquisite dishes.

"Sure," she assented, joyously, "but not here. Let's go around the corner to Joey's. I could get real chummy with a cup of good hot coffee and a ham on rye."

He helped her on with her coat, and if his hands rested a moment on her shoulders, who was there to see it? A few sleepy, wan-eyed waiters and Tillie, the scrub-woman. Together they started toward the door. Tillie, the scrub-woman, had worked her wet way out of the passage and into the kitchen proper. She and her pail blocked their way. She was sopping up a soapy pool with an all-encompassing gray scrub-rag. Heiny and Gussie stopped a moment perforce to watch her. It was rather fascinating to see how that artful scrub-rag craftily closed in upon the soapy pool until it engulfed it. Tillie sat back on her knees to wring out the water-soaked rag. There was something pleasing in the sight. Tillie's blue calico was faded white in patches and at the knees it was dark with soapy water. Her shoes were turned up ludicrously at the toes, as scrub-women's shoes always are. Tillie's thin hair was wadded back into a moist knob at the back and skewered with a gray-black hairpin. From her parboiled, shriveled fingers to her ruddy, perspiring face there was nothing of grace or beauty about Tillie. And yet Heiny found something pleasing there. He could not have told you why, so how can I, unless to say that it was, perhaps, for much the same reason that we rejoice in the wholesome, safe, reassuring feel of the gray woolen blanket on our bed when we wake from a horrid dream.

"A Happy New Year to you," said Heiny gravely, and took his hand out of his pocket.

Tillie's moist right hand closed over something. She smiled so that one saw all her broken black teeth.

"The same t' you," said Tillie. "The same t' you."

VI

One of the Old Girls

All of those ladies who end their conversation with you by wearily suggesting that you go down to the basement to find what you seek, do not receive a meager seven dollars a week as a reward for their efforts. Neither are they all obliged to climb five weary flights of stairs to reach the dismal little court room which is their home, and there are several who need not walk thirty-three blocks to save carfare, only to spend wretched evenings washing out handkerchiefs and stockings in the cracked little washbowl, while one ear is cocked for the stealthy tread of the Lady Who Objects.

The earnest compiler of working girls' budgets would pass Effie Bauer hurriedly by. Effie's budget bulged here and there with such pathetic items as hand-embroidered blouses, thick club steaks, and parquet tickets for Maude Adams. That you may visualize her at once I may say that Effie looked twenty-four—from the rear (all women do in these days of girlish simplicity in hats and tailor-mades); her skirts never sagged, her shirtwaists were marvels of plainness and fit, and her switch had cost her sixteen dollars, wholesale (a lady friend in the business). Oh, there was nothing tragic about Effie. She had a plump, assured style, a keen blue eye, a gift of repartee, and a way of doing her hair so that the gray at the sides scarcely showed at all. Also a knowledge of corsets that had placed her at the buying end of that important department at Spiegel's. Effie knew to the minute when coral beads went out and pearl beads came in, and just by looking at her blouses you could tell when Cluny died and Irish was born. Meeting Effie on the street, you would have put her down as one of the many well-dressed, prosperous-looking women shoppers—if you hadn't looked at her feet. Veteran clerks and policemen cannot disguise their feet.

Effie Bauer's reason for not marrying when a girl was the same as that of most of the capable, wise-eyed, good-looking women one finds at the head of departments. She had not had a chance. If Effie had been as attractive at twenty as she was at—there, we won't betray confidences. Still, it is certain that if Effie had been as attractive when a young girl as she was when an old girl, she never would have been an old girl and head of Spiegel's corset department at a salary of something very comfortably over one hundred and twenty-five a month (and commissions). Effie had improved with the years, and ripened with experience. She knew her value. At twenty she had been pale, anaemic and bony, with a startled-faun manner and bad teeth. Years of saleswomanship had broadened her, mentally and physically, until she possessed a wide and varied knowledge of that great and diversified subject known as human nature. She knew human nature all the way from the fifty-nine-cent girdles to the twenty-five-dollar made-to-orders. And if the years had brought, among other things, a certain hardness about the jaw and a line or two at the corners of the eyes, it was not surprising. You can't rub up against the sharp edges of this world and expect to come out without a scratch or so.

So much for Effie. Enter the hero. Webster defines a hero in romance as the person who has the principal share in the transactions related. He says nothing which would debar a gentleman just because he may be a trifle bald and in the habit of combing his hair over the thin spot, and he raises no objections to a matter of thickness and color in the region of the back of the neck. Therefore Gabe I. Marks qualifies. Gabe was the gentleman about whom Effie permitted herself to be guyed. He came to Chicago on business four times a year, and he always took Effie to the theater, and to supper afterward. On those occasions, Effie's gown, wrap and hat were as correct in texture, lines, and paradise aigrettes as those of any of her non-working sisters about her. On the morning following these excursions into Lobsterdom, Effie would confide to her friend, Miss Weinstein, of the lingeries and neligees:

"I was out with my friend, Mr. Marks, last evening. We went to Rector's after the show. Oh, well, it takes a New Yorker to know how. Honestly, I feel like a queen when I go out with him. H'm? Oh, nothing like that, girlie. I never could see that marriage thing. Just good friends."

Gabe had been coming to Chicago four times a year for six years. Six times four is twenty-four. And one is twenty-five. Gabe's last visit made the twenty-fifth.

"Well, Effie," Gabe said when the evening's entertainment had reached the restaurant stage, "this is our twenty-fifth anniversary. It's our silver wedding, without the silver and the wedding. We'll have a bottle of champagne. That makes it almost legal. And then suppose we finish up by having the wedding. The silver can be omitted."

Effie had been humming with the orchestra, holding a lobster claw in one hand and wielding the little two-pronged fork with the other. She dropped claw, fork, and popular air to stare open-mouthed at Gabe. Then a slow, uncertain smile crept about her lips, although her eyes were still unsmiling.

"Stop your joking, Gabie," she said. "Some day you'll say those things to the wrong lady, and then you'll have a breach-of-promise suit on your hands."

"This ain't no joke, Effie," Gabe had replied. "Not with me it ain't. As long as my Mother Selig lived I wouldn't ever marry a Goy. It would have broken her heart. I was a good son to her, and good sons make good husbands, they say. Well, Effie, you want to try it out?"

There was something almost solemn in Effie's tone and expression. "Gabie," she said slowly, "you're the first man that's ever asked me to marry him."

"That goes double," answered Gabe.

"Thanks," said Effie. "That makes it all the nicer."

"Then—" Gabe's face was radiant. But Effie shook her head quickly.

"You're just twenty years late," she said.

"Late!" expostulated Gabe. "I ain't no dead one yet."

Effie pushed her plate away with a little air of decision, folded her plump arms on the table, and, leaning forward, looked Gabe I. Marks squarely in the eyes.

"Gabie," she said gently, "I'll bet you haven't got a hundred dollars in the bank—"

"But—" interrupted Gabe.

"Wait a minute. I know you boys on the road. Besides your diamond scarf pin and your ring and watch, have you got a cent over your salary? Nix. You carry just about enough insurance to bury you, don't you? You're fifty years old if you're a minute, Gabie, and if I ain't mistaken you'd have a pretty hard time of it getting ten thousand dollars' insurance after the doctors got through with you. Twenty-five years of pinochle and poker and the fat of the land haven't added up any bumps in the old stocking under the mattress."

"Say, looka here," objected Gabe, more red-faced than usual, "I didn't know I was proposing to no Senatorial investigating committee. Say, you talk about them foreign noblemen being mercenary! Why, they ain't in it with you girls to-day. A feller is got to propose to you with his bank book in one hand and a bunch of life-insurance policies in the other. You're right; I ain't saved much. But Ma Selig always had everything she wanted. Say, when a man marries it's different. He begins to save."

"There!" said Effie quickly. "That's just it. Twenty years ago I'd have been glad and willing to start like that, saving and scrimping and loving a man, and looking forward to the time when four figures showed up in the bank account where but three bloomed before. I've got what they call the home instinct. Give me a yard or so of cretonne, and a photo of my married sister down in Iowa, and I can make even a boarding-house inside bedroom look like a place where a human being could live. If I had been as wise at twenty as I am now, Gabie, I could have married any man I pleased. But I was what they call capable. And men aren't marrying capable girls. They pick little yellow-headed, blue-eyed idiots that don't know a lamb stew from a soup bone when they see it. Well, Mr. Man didn't show up, and I started in to clerk at six per. I'm earning as much as you are now. More. Now, don't misunderstand me, Gabe. I'm not throwing bouquets at myself. I'm not that kind of a girl. But I could sell a style 743 Slimshape to the Venus de Milo herself. The Lord knows she needed one, with those hips of hers. I worked my way up, alone. I'm used to it. I like the excitement down at the store. I'm used to luxuries. I guess if I was a man I'd be the kind they call a good provider—the kind that opens wine every time there's half an excuse for it, and when he dies his widow has to take in boarders. And, Gabe, after you've worn tailored suits every year for a dozen years, you can't go back to twenty-five-dollar ready-mades and be happy."

"You could if you loved a man," said Gabe stubbornly.

The hard lines around the jaw and the experienced lines about the eyes seemed suddenly to stand out on Effie's face.

"Love's young dream is all right. But you've reached the age when you let your cigar ash dribble down onto your vest. Now me, I've got a kimono nature but a straight-front job, and it's kept me young. Young! I've got to be. That's my stock in trade. You see, Gabie, we're just twenty years late, both of us. They're not going to boost your salary. These days they're looking for kids on the road—live wires, with a lot of nerve and a quick come-back. They don't want old-timers. Why, say, Gabie, if I was to tell you what I spend in face powder and toilette water and hairpins alone, you'd think I'd made a mistake and given you the butcher bill instead. And I'm no professional beauty, either. Only it takes money to look cleaned and pressed in this town."

In the seclusion of the cafe corner, Gabe laid one plump, highly manicured hand on Effie's smooth arm. "You wouldn't need to stay young for me, Effie. I like you just as you are, without the powder, or the toilette water, or the hairpins."

His red, good-natured face had an expression upon it that was touchingly near patient resignation as he looked up into Effie's sparkling countenance. "You never looked so good to me as you do this minute, old girl. And if the day comes when you get lonesome—or change your mind—or—"

Effie shook her head, and started to draw on her long white gloves. "I guess I haven't refused you the way the dames in the novels do it. Maybe it's because I've had so little practice. But I want to say this, Gabe. Thank God I don't have to die knowing that no man ever wanted me to be his wife. Honestly, I'm that grateful that I'd marry you in a minute if I didn't like you so well."

"I'll be back in three months, like always," was all that Gabe said. "I ain't going to write. When I get here we'll just take in a show, and the younger you look the better I'll like it."

But on the occasion of Gabe's spring trip he encountered a statuesque blonde person where Effie had been wont to reign.

"Miss—er Bauer out of town?"

The statue melted a trifle in the sunshine of Gabe's ingratiating smile.

"Miss Bauer's ill," the statue informed him, using a heavy Eastern accent. "Anything I can do for you? I'm taking her place."

"Why—ah—not exactly; no," said Gabe. "Just a temporary indisposition, I suppose?"

"Well, you wouldn't hardly call it that, seeing that she's been sick with typhoid for seven weeks."

"Typhoid!" shouted Gabe.

"While I'm not in the habit of asking gentlemen their names, I'd like to inquire if yours happens to be Marks—Gabe I. Marks?"

"Sure," said Gabe. "That's me."

"Miss Bauer's nurse telephoned down last week that if a gentleman named Marks—Gabe I. Marks—drops in and inquires for Miss Bauer, I'm to tell him that she's changed her mind."

On the way from Spiegel's corset department to the car, Gabe stopped only for a bunch of violets. Effie's apartment house reached, he sent up his card, the violets, and a message that the gentleman was waiting. There came back a reply that sent Gabie up before the violets were relieved of their first layer of tissue paper.

Effie was sitting in a deep chair by the window, a flowered quilt bunched about her shoulders, her feet in gray knitted bedroom slippers. She looked every minute of her age, and she knew it, and didn't care. The hand that she held out to Gabe was a limp, white, fleshless thing that seemed to bear no relation to the plump, firm member that Gabe had pressed on so many previous occasions.

Gabe stared at this pale wraith in a moment of alarm and dismay. Then:

"You're looking—great!" he stammered. "Great! Nobody'd believe you'd been sick a minute. Guess you've just been stalling for a beauty rest, what?"

Effie smiled a tired little smile, and shook her head slowly.

"You're a good kid, Gabie, to lie like that just to make me feel good. But my nurse left yesterday and I had my first real squint at myself in the mirror. She wouldn't let me look while she was here. After what I saw staring back at me from that glass a whole ballroom full of French courtiers whispering sweet nothings in my ear couldn't make me believe that I look like anything but a hunk of Roquefort, green spots included. When I think of how my clothes won't fit it makes me shiver."

"Oh, you'll soon be back at the store as good as new. They fatten up something wonderful after typhoid. Why, I had a friend—"

"Did you get my message?" interrupted Effie.

"I was only talking to hide my nervousness," said Gabe, and started forward. But Effie waved him away.

"Sit down," she said. "I've got something to say." She looked thoughtfully down at one shining finger nail. Her lower lip was caught between her teeth. When she looked up again her eyes were swimming in tears. Gabe started forward again. Again Effie waved him away.

"It's all right, Gabie. I don't blubber as a rule. This fever leaves you as weak as a rag, and ready to cry if any one says 'Boo!' I've been doing some high-pressure thinking since nursie left. Had plenty of time to do it in, sitting here by this window all day. My land! I never knew there was so much time. There's been days when I haven't talked to a soul, except the nurse and the chambermaid. Lonesome! Say, the amount of petting I could stand would surprise you. Of course, my nurse was a perfectly good nurse—at twenty-five per. But I was just a case to her. You can't expect a nurse to ooze sympathy over an old maid with the fever. I tell you I was dying to have some one say 'Sh-sh-sh!' when there was a noise, just to show they were interested. Whenever I'd moan the nurse would come over and stick a thermometer in my mouth and write something down on a chart. The boys and girls at the store sent flowers. They'd have done the same if I'd died. When the fever broke I just used to lie there and dream, not feeling anything in particular, and not caring much whether it was day or night. Know what I mean?"

Gabie shook a sympathetic head.

There was a little silence. Then Effie went on. "I used to think I was pretty smart, earning my own good living, dressing as well as the next one, and able to spend my vacation in Atlantic City if I wanted to. I didn't know I was missing anything. But while I was sick I got to wishing that there was somebody that belonged to me. Somebody to worry about me, and to sit up nights—somebody that just naturally felt they had to come tiptoeing into my room every three or four minutes to see if I was sleeping, or had enough covers on, or wanted a drink, or something. I got to thinking what it would have been like if I had a husband and a—home. You'll think I'm daffy, maybe."

Gabie took Effie's limp white hand in his, and stroked it gently. Effie's face was turned away from him, toward the noisy street.

"I used to imagine how he'd come home at six, stamping his feet, maybe, and making a lot of noise the way men do. And then he'd remember, and come creaking up the steps, and he'd stick his head in at the door in the funny, awkward, pathetic way men have in a sick room. And he'd say, 'How's the old girl to-night? I'd better not come near you now, puss, because I'll bring the cold with me. Been lonesome for your old man?'

"And I'd say, 'Oh, I don't care how cold you are, dear. The nurse is downstairs, getting my supper ready.'

"And then he'd come tiptoeing over to my bed, and stoop down, and kiss me, and his face would be all cold, and rough, and his mustache would be wet, and he'd smell out-doorsy and smoky, the way husbands do when they come in. And I'd reach up and pat his cheek and say, 'You need a shave, old man.'

"'I know it,' he'd say, rubbing his cheek up against mine.

"'Hurry up and wash, now. Supper'll be ready.'

"'Where are the kids?' he'd ask. 'The house is as quiet as the grave. Hurry up and get well, kid. It's darn lonesome without you at the table, and the children's manners are getting something awful, and I never can find my shirts. Lordy, I guess we won't celebrate when you get up! Can't you eat a little something nourishing for supper—beefsteak, or a good plate of soup, or something?'

"Men are like that, you know. So I'd say then: 'Run along, you old goose! You'll be suggesting sauerkraut and wieners next. Don't you let Millie have any marmalade to-night. She's got a spoiled stomach.'

"And then he'd pound off down the hall to wash up, and I'd shut my eyes, and smile to myself, and everything would be all right, because he was home."

There was a long silence. Effie's eyes were closed. But two great tears stole out from beneath each lid and coursed their slow way down her thin cheeks. She did not raise her hand to wipe them away.

Gabie's other hand reached over and met the one that already clasped Effie's.

"Effie," he said, in a voice that was as hoarse as it was gentle.

"H'm?" said Effie.

"Will you marry me?"

"I shouldn't wonder," replied Effie, opening her eyes. "No, don't kiss me. You might catch something. But say, reach up and smooth my hair away from my forehead, will you, and call me a couple of fool names. I don't care how clumsy you are about it. I could stand an awful fuss being made over me, without being spoiled any."

Three weeks later Effie was back at the store. Her skirt didn't fit in the back, and the little hollow places in her cheeks did not take the customary dash of rouge as well as when they had been plumper. She held a little impromptu reception that extended down as far as the lingeries and up as far as the rugs. The old sparkle came back to Effie's eye. The old assurance and vigor seemed to return. By the time that Miss Weinstein, of the French lingeries, arrived, breathless, to greet her Effie was herself again.

"Well, if you're not a sight for sore eyes, dearie," exclaimed Miss Weinstein. "My goodness, how grand and thin you are! I'd be willing to take a course in typhoid myself, if I thought I could lose twenty-five pounds."

"I haven't a rag that fits me," Effie announced proudly.

Miss Weinstein lowered her voice discreetly. "Dearie, can you come down to my department for a minute? We're going to have a sale on imported lawnjerie blouses, slightly soiled, from nine to eleven to-morrow. There's one you positively must see. Hand-embroidered, Irish motifs, and eyeleted from soup to nuts, and only eight-fifty."

"I've got a fine chance of buying hand-made waists, no matter how slightly soiled," Effie made answer, "with a doctor and nurse's bill as long as your arm."

"Oh, run along!" scoffed Miss Weinstein. "A person would think you had a husband to get a grouch every time you get reckless to the extent of a new waist. You're your own boss. And you know your credit's good. Honestly, it would be a shame to let this chance slip. You're not getting tight in your old age, are you?"

"N-no," faltered Effie, "but—"

"Then come on," urged Miss Weinstein energetically. "And be thankful you haven't got a man to raise the dickens when the bill comes in."

"Do you mean that?" asked Effie slowly, fixing Miss Weinstein with a thoughtful eye.

"Surest thing you know. Say, girlie, let's go over to Klein's for lunch this noon. They have pot roast with potato pfannkuchen on Tuesdays, and we can split an order between us."

"Hold that waist till to-morrow, will you?" said Effie. "I've made an arrangement with a—friend that might make new clothes impossible just now. But I'm going to wire my party that the arrangement is all off. I've changed my mind. I ought to get an answer to-morrow. Did you say it was a thirty-six?"

VII

Maymeys from Cuba

There is nothing new in this. It has all been done before. But tell me, what is new? Does the aspiring and perspiring summer vaudeville artist flatter himself that his stuff is going big? Then does the stout man with the oyster-colored eyelids in the first row, left, turn his bullet head on his fat-creased neck to remark huskily to his companion:

"The hook for him. R-r-r-rotten! That last one was an old Weber 'n, Fields gag. They discarded it back in '91. Say, the good ones is all dead, anyhow. Take old Salvini, now, and Dan Rice. Them was actors. Come on out and have something."

Does the short-story writer felicitate himself upon having discovered a rare species in humanity's garden? The Blase Reader flips the pages between his fingers, yawns, stretches, and remarks to his wife:

"That's a clean lift from Kipling—or is it Conan Doyle? Anyway, I've read something just like it before. Say, kid, guess what these magazine guys get for a full page ad? Nix. That's just like a woman. Three thousand straight. Fact."

To anticipate the delver into the past it may be stated that the plot of this one originally appeared in the Eternal Best Seller, under the heading, "He Asked You for Bread, and Ye Gave Him a Stone." There may be those who could not have traced my plagiarism to its source.

Although the Book has had an unprecedentedly long run it is said to be less widely read than of yore.

Even with this preparation I hesitate to confess that this is the story of a hungry girl in a big city. Well, now, wait a minute. Conceding that it has been done by every scribbler from tyro to best seller expert, you will acknowledge that there is the possibility of a fresh viewpoint— twist—what is it the sporting editors call it? Oh, yes—slant. There is the possibility of getting a new slant on an old idea. That may serve to deflect the line of the deadly parallel.

Just off State Street there is a fruiterer and importer who ought to be arrested for cruelty. His window is the most fascinating and the most heartless in Chicago. A line of open-mouthed, wide-eyed gazers is always to be found before it. Despair, wonder, envy, and rebellion smolder in the eyes of those gazers. No shop window show should be so diabolically set forth as to arouse such sensations in the breast of the beholder. It is a work of art, that window; a breeder of anarchism, a destroyer of contentment, a second feast of Tantalus. It boasts peaches, dewy and golden, when peaches have no right to be; plethoric, purple bunches of English hothouse grapes are there to taunt the ten-dollar-a-week clerk whose sick wife should be in the hospital; strawberries glow therein when shortcake is a last summer's memory, and forced cucumbers remind us that we are taking ours in the form of dill pickles. There is, perhaps, a choice head of cauliflower, so exquisite in its ivory and green perfection as to be fit for a bride's bouquet; there are apples so flawless that if the Garden of Eden grew any as perfect it is small wonder that Eve fell for them.

There are fresh mushrooms, and jumbo cocoanuts, and green almonds; costly things in beds of cotton nestle next to strange and marvelous things in tissue wrappings. Oh, that window is no place for the hungry, the dissatisfied, or the man out of a job. When the air is filled with snow there is that in the sight of muskmelons which incites crime.

Queerly enough, the gazers before that window foot up the same, year in, and year out, something after this fashion:

Item: One anemic little milliner's apprentice in coat and shoes that even her hat can't redeem.

Item: One sandy-haired, gritty-complexioned man, with a drooping ragged mustache, a tin dinner bucket, and lime on his boots.

Item: One thin mail carrier with an empty mail sack, gaunt cheeks, and an habitual droop to his left shoulder.

Item: One errand boy troubled with a chronic sniffle, a shrill and piping whistle, and a great deal of shuffling foot-work.

Item: One negro wearing a spotted tan topcoat, frayed trousers and no collar. His eyes seem all whites as he gazes.

Enough of the window. But bear it in mind while we turn to Jennie. Jennie's real name was Janet, and she was Scotch. Canny? Not necessarily, or why should she have been hungry and out of a job in January?

Jennie stood in the row before the window, and stared. The longer she stared the sharper grew the lines that fright and under-feeding had chiseled about her nose, and mouth, and eyes. When your last meal is an eighteen-hour-old memory, and when that memory has only near-coffee and a roll to dwell on, there is something in the sight of January peaches and great strawberries carelessly spilling out of a tipped box, just like they do in the fruit picture on the dining-room wall, that is apt to carve sharp lines in the corners of the face.

The tragic line dwindled, going about its business. The man with the dinner pail and the lime on his boots spat, drew the back of his hand across his mouth, and turned away with an ugly look. (Pork was up to $14.25, dressed.)

The errand boy's blithe whistle died down to a mournful dirge.

He was window-wishing. His choice wavered between the juicy pears, and the foreign-looking red things that looked like oranges, and weren't. One hand went into his coat pocket, extracting an apple that was to have formed the pièce de résistance of his noonday lunch. Now he regarded it with a sort of pitying disgust, and bit into it with the middle-of-the-morning contempt that it deserved.

The mail carrier pushed back his cap and reflectively scratched his head. How much over his month's wage would that green basket piled high with exotic fruit come to?

Jennie stood and stared after they had left and another line had formed. If you could have followed her gaze with dotted lines, as they do in the cartoons, you would have seen that it was not the peaches, or the prickly pears, or the strawberries, or the muskmelon or even the grapes, that held her eye. In the center of that wonderful window was an oddly woven basket. In the basket were brown things that looked like sweet potatoes. One knew that they were not. A sign over the basket informed the puzzled gazer that these were maymeys from Cuba.

Maymeys from Cuba. The humor of it might have struck Jennie if she had not been so Scotch, and so hungry. As it was, a slow, sullen, heavy Scotch wrath rose in her breast. Maymeys from Cuba.

The wantonness of it! Peaches? Yes. Grapes, even, and pears and cherries in snow time. But maymeys from Cuba—why, one did not even know if they were to be eaten with butter, or with vinegar, or in the hand, like an apple. Who wanted maymeys from Cuba? They had gone all those hundreds of miles to get a fruit or vegetable thing—a thing so luxurious, so out of all reason that one did not know whether it was to be baked, or eaten raw. There they lay, in their foreign-looking basket, taunting Jennie who needed a quarter.

Have I told you how Jennie happened to be hungry and jobless? Well, then I sha'n't. It doesn't really matter, anyway. The fact is enough. If you really demand to know you might inquire of Mr. Felix Klein. You will find him in a mahogany office on the sixth floor. The door is marked manager. It was his idea to import Scotch lassies from Dunfermline for his Scotch linen department. The idea was more fetching than feasible.

There are people who will tell you that no girl possessing a grain of common sense and a little nerve need go hungry, no matter how great the city. Don't you believe them. The city has heard the cry of wolf so often that it refuses to listen when he is snarling at the door, particularly when the door is next door.

Where did we leave Jennie? Still standing on the sidewalk before the fruit and fancy goods shop, gazing at the maymeys from Cuba. Finally her Scotch bump of curiosity could stand it no longer. She dug her elbow into the arm of the person standing next in line.

"What are those?" she asked.

The next in line happened to be a man. He was a man without an overcoat, and with his chin sunk deep into his collar, and his hands thrust deep into his pockets. It looked as though he were trying to crawl inside himself for warmth.

"Those? That sign says they're maymeys from Cuba."

"I know," persisted Jennie, "but what are they?"

"Search me. Say, I ain't bothering about maymeys from Cuba. A couple of hot murphies from Ireland, served with a lump of butter, would look good enough to me."

"Do you suppose any one buys them?" marveled Jennie.

"Surest thing you know. Some rich dame coming by here, wondering what she can have for dinner to tempt the jaded palates of her dear ones, see? She sees them Cuban maymeys. 'The very thing!' she says. 'I'll have 'em served just before the salad.' And she sails in and buys a pound or two. I wonder, now, do you eat 'em with a fruit knife, or with a spoon?"

Jennie took one last look at the woven basket with its foreign contents. Then she moved on, slowly. She had been moving on for hours—weeks.

Most people have acquired the habit of eating three meals a day. In a city of some few millions the habit has made necessary the establishing of many thousands of eating places. Jennie would have told you that there were billions of these. To her the world seemed composed of one huge, glittering restaurant, with myriads of windows through which one caught maddening glimpses of ketchup bottles, and nickel coffee heaters, and piles of doughnuts, and scurrying waiters in white, and people critically studying menu cards. She walked in a maze of restaurants, cafes, eating-houses. Tables and diners loomed up at every turn, on every street, from Michigan Avenue's rose-shaded Louis the Somethingth palaces, where every waiter owns his man, to the white tile mausoleums where every man is his own waiter. Everywhere there were windows full of lemon cream pies, and pans of baked apples swimming in lakes of golden syrup, and pots of baked beans with the pink and crispy slices of pork just breaking through the crust. Every dairy lunch mocked one with the sign of "wheat cakes with maple syrup and country sausage, 20 cents."

There are those who will say that for cases like Jennie's there are soup kitchens, Y.W.C.A.s, relief associations, policemen, and things like that. And so there are. Unfortunately, the people who need them aren't up on them. Try it. Plant yourself, penniless, in the middle of State Street on a busy day, dive into the howling, scrambling, pushing maelstrom that hurls itself against the mountainous and impregnable form of the crossing policeman, and see what you'll get out of it, provided you have the courage.

Desperation gave Jennie a false courage. On the strength of it she made two false starts. The third time she reached the arm of the crossing policeman, and clutched it. That imposing giant removed the whistle from his mouth, and majestically inclined his head without turning his gaze upon Jennie, one eye being fixed on a red automobile that was showing signs of sulking at its enforced pause, the other being busy with a cursing drayman who was having an argument with his off horse.

Jennie mumbled her question.

Said the crossing policeman:

"Getcher car on Wabash, ride to 'umpty-second, transfer, get off at Blank Street, and walk three blocks south."

Then he put the whistle back in his mouth, blew two shrill blasts, and the horde of men, women, motors, drays, trucks, cars, and horses swept over him, through him, past him, leaving him miraculously untouched.

Jennie landed on the opposite curbing, breathing hard. What was that street? Umpty-what? Well, it didn't matter, anyway. She hadn't the nickel for car fare.

What did you do next? You begged from people on the street. Jennie selected a middle-aged, prosperous, motherly looking woman. She framed her plea with stiff lips. Before she had finished her sentence she found herself addressing empty air. The middle-aged, prosperous, motherly looking woman had hurried on.

Well, then you tried a man. You had to be careful there. He mustn't be the wrong kind. There were so many wrong kinds. Just an ordinary looking family man would be best. Ordinary looking family men are strangely in the minority. There are so many more bull-necked, tan-shoed ones. Finally Jennie's eye, grown sharp with want, saw one. Not too well dressed, kind-faced, middle-aged.

She fell into step beside him.

"Please, can you help me out with a shilling?"

Jennie's nose was red, and her eyes watery. Said the middle-aged family man with the kindly face:

"Beat it. You've had about enough, I guess."

Jennie walked into a department store, picked out the oldest and most stationary looking floorwalker, and put it to him. The floorwalker bent his head, caught the word "food," swung about, and pointed over Jennie's head.

"Grocery department on the seventh floor. Take one of those elevators up."

Any one but a floorwalker could have seen the misery in Jennie's face. But to floorwalkers all women's faces are horrible.

Jennie turned and walked blindly toward the elevators. There was no fight left in her. If the floorwalker had said, "Silk negligees on the fourth floor. Take one of those elevators up," Jennie would have ridden up to the fourth floor, and stupidly gazed at pink silk and Val lace negligees in glass cases.

Tell me, have you ever visited the grocery department of a great store on the wrong side of State Street? It's a mouth-watering experience. A department store grocery is a glorified mixture of delicatessen shop, meat market, and vaudeville. Starting with the live lobsters and crabs you work your hungry way right around past the cheeses, and the sausages, and the hams, and tongues, and head-cheese, past the blonde person in white who makes marvelous and uneatable things out of gelatine, through a thousand smells and scents—smells of things smoked, and pickled, and spiced, and baked and preserved, and roasted.

Jennie stepped out of the elevator, licking her lips. She sniffed the air, eagerly, as a hound sniffs the scent. She shut her eyes when she passed the sugar-cured hams. A woman was buying a slice from one, and the butcher was extolling its merits. Jennie caught the words "juicy" and "corn-fed."

That particular store prides itself on its cheese department. It boasts that there one can get anything in cheese from the simple cottage variety to imposing mottled Stilton. There are cheeses from France, cheeses from Switzerland, cheeses from Holland. Brick and parmesan, Edam and Limburger perfumed the atmosphere.

Behind the counters were big, full-fed men in white aprons, and coats. They flourished keen bright knives. As Jennie gazed, one of them, in a moment of idleness, cut a tiny wedge from a rich yellow Swiss cheese and stood nibbling it absently, his eyes wandering toward the blonde gelatine demonstrator. Jennie swayed, and caught the counter. She felt horribly faint and queer. She shut her eyes for a moment. When she opened them a woman—a fat, housewifely, comfortable looking woman—was standing before the cheese counter. She spoke to the cheese man. Once more his sharp knife descended and he was offering the possible customer a sample. She picked it off the knife's sharp tip, nibbled thoughtfully, shook her head, and passed on. A great, glorious world of hope opened out before Jennie.

Her cheeks grew hot, and her eyes felt dry and bright as she approached the cheese counter.

"A bit of that," she said, pointing. "It doesn't look just as I like it."

"Very fine, madam," the man assured her, and turned the knife point toward her, with the infinitesimal wedge of cheese reposing on its blade. Jennie tried to keep her hand steady as she delicately picked it off, nibbled as she had seen that other woman do it, her head on one side, before it shook a slow negative. The effort necessary to keep from cramming the entire piece into her mouth at once left her weak and trembling. She passed on as the other woman had done, around the corner, and into a world of sausages. Great rosy mounds of them filled counters and cases. Sausage! Sneer, you pâté de foie grasers! But may you know the day when hunger will have you. And on that day may you run into linked temptation in the form of Braunschweiger Metwurst. May you know the longing that causes the eyes to glaze at the sight of Thuringer sausage, and the mouth to water at the scent of Cervelat wurst, and the fingers to tremble at the nearness of smoked liver.

Jennie stumbled on, through the smells and the sights. That nibble of cheese had been like a drop of human blood to a man-eating tiger. It made her bold, cunning, even while it maddened. She stopped at this counter and demanded a slice of summer sausage. It was paper-thin, but delicious beyond belief. At the next counter there was corned beef, streaked fat and lean. Jennie longed to bury her teeth in the succulent meat and get one great, soul-satisfying mouthful. She had to be content with her judicious nibbling. To pass the golden-brown, breaded pig's feet was torture. To look at the codfish balls was agony. And so Jennie went on, sampling, tasting, the scraps of food acting only as an aggravation. Up one aisle, and down the next she went. And then, just around the corner, she brought up before the grocery department's pride and boast, the Scotch bakery. It is the store's star vaudeville feature. All day long the gaping crowd stands before it, watching David the Scone Man, as with sleeves rolled high above his big arms, he kneads, and slaps, and molds, and thumps and shapes the dough into toothsome Scotch confections. There was a crowd around the white counters now, and the flat baking surface of the gas stove was just hot enough, and David the Scone Man (he called them Scuns) was whipping about here and there, turning the baking oat cakes, filling the shelf above the stove when they were done to a turn, rolling out fresh ones, waiting on customers. His nut-cracker face almost allowed itself a pleased expression—but not quite. David the Scone Man was Scotch (I was going to add, d'ye ken, but I will not).

Jennie wondered if she really saw those things. Mutton pies! Scones! Scotch short bread! Oat cakes! She edged closer, wriggling her way through the little crowd until she stood at the counter's edge. David the Scone Man, his back to the crowd, was turning the last batch of oat cakes. Jennie felt strangely light-headed, and unsteady, and airy. She stared straight ahead, a half-smile on her lips, while a hand that she knew was her own, and that yet seemed no part of her, stole out, very, very slowly, and cunningly, and extracted a hot scone from the pile that lay in the tray on the counter. That hand began to steal back, more quickly now. But not quickly enough. Another hand grasped her wrist. A woman's high, shrill voice (why will women do these things to each other?) said, excitedly:

"'Say, Scone Man! Scone Man! This girl is stealing something!'"

A buzz of exclamations from the crowd—a closing in upon her—a whirl of faces, and counter, and trays, and gas stove. Jennie dropped with a crash, the warm scone still grasped in her fingers.

Just before the ambulance came it was the blonde lady of the impossible gelatines who caught the murmur that came from Jennie's white lips. The blonde lady bent her head closer. Closer still. When she raised her face to those other faces crowded near, her eyes were round with surprise.

"'S far's I can make out, she says her name's Mamie, and she's from Cuba. Well, wouldn't that eat you! I always thought they was dark complected."

VIII

The Leading Lady

The leading lady lay on her bed and wept. Not as you have seen leading ladies weep, becomingly, with eyebrows pathetically V-shaped, mouth quivering, sequined bosom heaving. The leading lady lay on her bed in a red-and-blue-striped kimono and wept as a woman weeps, her head burrowing into the depths of the lumpy hotel pillow, her teeth biting the pillow-case to choke back the sounds so that the grouch in the next room might not hear.

Presently the leading lady's right hand began to grope about on the bedspread for her handkerchief. Failing to find it, she sat up wearily, raising herself on one elbow and pushing her hair back from her forehead—not as you have seen a leading lady pass a lily hand across her alabaster brow, but as a heart-sick woman does it. Her tears and sniffles had formed a little oasis of moisture on the pillow's white bosom so that the ugly stripe of the ticking showed through. She gazed down at the damp circle with smarting, swollen eyes, and another lump came up into her throat.

Then she sat up resolutely, and looked about her. The leading lady had a large and saving sense of humor. But there is nothing that blunts the sense of humor more quickly than a few months of one-night stands. Even O. Henry could have seen nothing funny about that room.

The bed was of green enamel, with fly-specked gold trimmings. It looked like a huge frog. The wall-paper was a crime. It represented an army of tan mustard plasters climbing up a chocolate-fudge wall. The leading lady was conscious of a feeling of nausea as she gazed at it. So she got up and walked to the window. The room faced west, and the hot afternoon sun smote full on her poor swollen eyes. Across the street the red brick walls of the engine-house caught the glare and sent it back. The firemen, in their blue shirt-sleeves, were seated in the shade before the door, their chairs tipped at an angle of sixty. The leading lady stared down into the sun-baked street, turned abruptly and made as though to fall upon the bed again, with a view to forming another little damp oasis on the pillow. But when she reached the center of the stifling little bedroom her eye chanced on the electric call-button near the door. Above the electric bell was tacked a printed placard giving information on the subjects of laundry, ice-water, bell-boys and dining-room hours.

The leading lady stood staring at it a moment thoughtfully. Then with a sudden swift movement she applied her forefinger to the button and held it there for a long half-minute. Then she sat down on the edge of the bed, her kimono folded about her, and waited.

She waited until a lank bell-boy, in a brown uniform that was some sizes too small for him, had ceased to take any interest in the game of chess which Bauer and Merkle, the champion firemen chess-players, were contesting on the walk before the open doorway of the engine-house. The proprietor of the Burke House had originally intended that the brown uniform be worn by a diminutive bell-boy, such as one sees in musical comedies. But the available supply of stage size bell-boys in our town is somewhat limited and was soon exhausted. There followed a succession of lank bell-boys, with arms and legs sticking ungracefully out of sleeves and trousers.

"Come!" called the leading lady quickly, in answer to the lank youth's footsteps, and before he had had time to knock.

"Ring?" asked the boy, stepping into the torrid little room.

The leading lady did not reply immediately. She swallowed something in her throat and pushed back the hair from her moist forehead again. The brown uniform repeated his question, a trifle irritably. Whereupon the leading lady spoke, desperately:

"Is there a woman around this place? I don't mean dining-room girls, or the person behind the cigar-counter."

Since falling heir to the brown uniform the lank youth had heard some strange requests. He had been interviewed by various ladies in varicolored kimonos relative to liquid refreshment, laundry and the cost of hiring a horse and rig for a couple of hours. One had even summoned him to ask if there was a Bible in the house. But this latest question was a new one. He stared, leaning against the door and thrusting one hand into the depths of his very tight breeches pocket.

"Why, there's Pearlie Schultz," he said at last, with a grin.

"Who's she?" The leading lady sat up expectantly.

"Steno."

The expectant figure drooped. "Blonde? And Irish crochet collar with a black velvet bow on her chest?"

"Who? Pearlie? Naw. You mustn't get Pearlie mixed with the common or garden variety of stenos. Pearlie is fat, and she wears specs and she's got a double chin. Her hair is skimpy and she don't wear no rat. W'y no traveling man has ever tried to flirt with Pearlie yet. Pearlie's what you'd call a woman, all right. You wouldn't never make a mistake and think she'd escaped from the first row in the chorus."

The leading lady rose from the bed, reached out for her pocket-book, extracted a dime, and held it out to the bell-boy.

"Here. Will you ask her to come up here to me? Tell her I said please."

After he had gone she seated herself on the edge of the bed again, with a look in her eyes like that which you have seen in the eyes of a dog that is waiting for a door to be opened.

Fifteen minutes passed. The look in the eyes of the leading lady began to fade. Then a footstep sounded down the hall. The leading lady cocked her head to catch it, and smiled blissfully. It was a heavy, comfortable footstep, under which a board or two creaked. There came a big, sensible thump-thump-thump at the door, with stout knuckles. The leading lady flew to answer it. She flung the door wide and stood there, clutching her kimono at the throat and looking up into a red, good-natured face.

Pearlie Schultz looked down at the leading lady kindly and benignantly, as a mastiff might look at a terrier.

"Lonesome for a bosom to cry on?" asked she, and stepped into the room, walked to the west windows, and jerked down the shades with a zip-zip, shutting off the yellow glare. She came back to where the leading lady was standing and patted her on the cheek, lightly.

"You tell me all about it," said she, smiling.

The leading lady opened her lips, gulped, tried again, gulped again—Pearlie Schultz shook a sympathetic head.

"Ain't had a decent, close-to-nature powwow with a woman for weeks and weeks, have you?"

"How did you know?" cried the leading lady.

"You've got that hungry look. There was a lady drummer here last winter, and she had the same expression. She was so dead sick of eating her supper and then going up to her ugly room and reading and sewing all evening that it was a wonder she'd stayed good. She said it was easy

81

enough for the men. They could smoke, and play pool, and go to a show, and talk to any one that looked good to 'em. But if she tried to amuse herself everybody'd say she was tough. She cottoned to me like a burr to a wool skirt. She traveled for a perfumery house, and she said she hadn't talked to a woman, except the dry-goods clerks who were nice to her trying to work her for her perfume samples, for weeks an' weeks. Why, that woman made crochet by the bolt, and mended her clothes evenings whether they needed it or not, and read till her eyes come near going back on her."

The leading lady seized Pearlie's hand and squeezed it.

"That's it! Why, I haven't talked—really talked—to a real woman since the company went out on the road. I'm leading lady of the 'Second Wife' company, you know. It's one of those small cast plays, with only five people in it. I play the wife, and I'm the only woman in the cast. It's terrible. I ought to be thankful to get the part these days. And I was, too. But I didn't know it would be like this. I'm going crazy. The men in the company are good kids, but I can't go trailing around after them all day. Besides, it wouldn't be right. They're all married, except Billy, who plays the kid, and he's busy writing a vaudeville skit that he thinks the New York managers are going to fight for when he gets back home. We were to play Athens, Wisconsin, to-night, but the house burned down night before last, and that left us with an open date. When I heard the news you'd have thought I had lost my mother. It's bad enough having a whole day to kill but when I think of to-night," the leading lady's voice took on a note of hysteria, "it seems as though I'd—"

"Say," Pearlie interrupted, abruptly, "you ain't got a real good corset-cover pattern, have you? One that fits smooth over the bust and don't slip off the shoulders? I don't seem able to get my hands on the kind I want."

"Have I!" yelled the leading lady. And made a flying leap from the bed to the floor.

She flapped back the cover of a big suit-case and began burrowing into its depths, strewing the floor with lingerie, newspaper clippings, blouses, photographs and Dutch collars. Pearlie came over and sat down on the floor in the midst of the litter. The leading lady dived once more, fished about in the bottom of the suit-case and brought a crumpled piece of paper triumphantly to the surface.

"This is it. It only takes a yard and five-eighths. And fits! Like Anna Held's skirts. Comes down in a V front and back—like this. See? And no fulness. Wait a minute. I'll show you my princess slip. I made it all by hand, too. I'll bet you couldn't buy it under fifteen dollars, and it cost me four dollars and eighty cents, with the lace and all."

Before an hour had passed, the leading lady had displayed all her treasures, from the photograph of her baby that died to her new Blanche Ring curl cluster, and was calling Pearlie by her first name. When a bell somewhere boomed six o'clock Pearlie was being instructed in a new exercise calculated to reduce the hips an inch a month.

"My land!" cried Pearlie, aghast, and scrambled to her feet as nimbly as any woman can who weighs two hundred pounds. "Supper-time, and I've got a bunch of letters an inch thick to get out! I'd better reduce that some before I begin on my hips. But say, I've had a lovely time."

The leading lady clung to her. "You've saved my life. Why, I forgot all about being hot and lonely and a couple of thousand miles from New York. Must you go?"

"Got to. But if you'll promise you won't laugh, I'll make a date for this evening that'll give you a new sensation anyway. There's going to be a strawberry social on the lawn of the parsonage of our church. I've got a booth. You shed that kimono, and put on a thin dress and those curls and some powder, and I'll introduce you as my friend, Miss Evans. You don't look Evans, but this is a Methodist church strawberry festival, and if I was to tell them that you are leading lady of the 'Second Wife' company they'd excommunicate my booth."

"A strawberry social!" gasped the leading lady. "Do they still have them?" She did not laugh. "Why, I used to go to strawberry festivals when I was a little girl in—"

"Careful! You'll be giving away your age, and, anyway, you don't look it. Fashions in strawberry socials ain't changed much. Better bathe your eyes in eau de cologne or whatever it is they're always dabbing on 'em in books. See you at eight."

At eight o'clock Pearlie's thump-thump sounded again, and the leading lady sprang to the door as before. Pearlie stared. This was no tear-stained, heat-bedraggled creature in an unbecoming red-striped kimono. It was a remarkably pretty woman in a white lingerie gown over a pink slip. The leading lady knew a thing or two about the gentle art of making-up!

"That just goes to show," remarked Pearlie, "that you must never judge a woman in a kimono or a bathing suit. You look nineteen. Say, I forgot something down-stairs. Just get your handkerchief and chamois together and meet in my cubbyhole next to the lobby, will you? I'll be ready for you."

Down-stairs she summoned the lank bell-boy. "You go outside and tell Sid Strang I want to see him, will you? He's on the bench with the baseball bunch."

Pearlie had not seen Sid Strang outside. She did not need to. She knew he was there. In our town all the young men dress up in their pale gray suits and lavender-striped shirts after supper on summer evenings. Then they stroll down to the Burke House, buy a cigar and sit down on the benches in front of the hotel to talk baseball and watch the girls go by. It is astonishing to note the number of our girls who have letters to mail after supper. One would think that they must drive their pens fiercely all the afternoon in order to get out such a mass of correspondence.

The obedient Sid reached the door of Pearlie's little office just off the lobby as the leading lady came down the stairs with a spangled scarf trailing over her arm. It was an effective entrance.

"Why, hello!" said Pearlie, looking up from her typewriter as though Sid Strang were the last person in the world she expected to see. "What do you want here? Ethel, this is my friend, Mr. Sid Strang, one of our rising young lawyers. His neckties always match his socks. Sid, this is my friend, Miss Ethel Evans, of New York. We're going over to the strawberry social at the M. E. parsonage. I don't suppose you'd care about going?"

Mr. Sid Strang gazed at the leading lady in the white lingerie dress with the pink slip, and the V-shaped neck, and the spangled scarf, and turned to Pearlie.

"Why, Pearlie Schultz!" he said reproachfully. "How can you ask? You know what a strawberry social means to me! I haven't missed one in years!"

"I know it," replied Pearlie, with a grin. "You feel the same way about Thursday evening prayer-meeting too, don't you? You can walk over with us if you want to. We're going now. Miss Evans and I have got a booth."

Sid walked. Pearlie led them determinedly past the rows of gray suits and lavender and pink shirts on the benches in front of the hotel. And as the leading lady came into view the gray suits stopped talking baseball and sat up and took notice. Pearlie had known all those young men inside of the swagger suits in the days when their summer costume consisted of a pair of dad's pants cut down to a doubtful fit, and a non-descript shirt damp from the swimming-hole. So she called out, cheerily:

"We're going over to the strawberry festival. I expect to see all you boys there to contribute your mite to the church carpet."

The leading lady turned to look at them, and smiled. They were such a dapper, pink-cheeked, clean-looking lot of boys, she thought. At that the benches rose to a man and announced that they might as well stroll over right now. Whenever a new girl comes to visit in our town our boys make a concerted rush at her, and develop a "case" immediately, and the girl goes home when her visit is over with her head swimming, and forever after bores the girls of her home town with tales of her conquests.

The ladies of the First M. E. Church still talk of the money they garnered at the strawberry festival. Pearlie's out-of-town friend was garnerer-in-chief. You take a cross-eyed, pock-marked girl and put her in a white dress, with a pink slip, on a green lawn under a string of rose-colored Japanese lanterns, and she'll develop an almost Oriental beauty. It is an ideal setting. The leading lady was not cross-eyed or pock-marked. She stood at the lantern-illumined booth, with Pearlie in the background, and dispensed an unbelievable amount of strawberries. Sid Strang and the hotel bench brigade assisted. They made engagements to take Pearlie and her friend down to the river next day, and to the ball game, and planned innumerable picnics, gazing meanwhile into the leading lady's eyes. There grew in the cheeks of the leading lady a flush that was not brought about by the pink slip, or the Japanese lanterns, or the skillful application of rouge.

By nine o'clock the strawberry supply was exhausted, and the president of the Foreign Missionary Society was sending wildly down-town for more ice-cream.

"I call it an outrage," puffed Pearlie happily, ladling ice-cream like mad. "Making a poor working girl like me slave all evening! How many was that last order? Four? My land! that's the third dish of ice-cream Ed White's had! You'll have something to tell the villagers about when you get back to New York."

The leading lady turned a flushed face toward Pearlie. "This is more fun than the Actors' Fair. I had the photograph booth last year, and I took in nearly as much as Lil Russell; and goodness knows, all she needs to do at a fair is to wear her diamond-and-pearl stomacher and her set-piece smile, and the men just swarm around her like the pictures of a crowd in a McCutcheon cartoon."

When the last Japanese lantern had guttered out, Pearlie Schultz and the leading lady prepared to go home. Before they left, the M. E. ladies came over to Pearlie's booth and personally congratulated the leading lady, and thanked her for the interest she had taken in the cause, and the secretary of the Epworth League asked her to come to the tea that was to be held at her home the following Tuesday. The leading lady thanked her and said she'd come if she could.

Escorted by a bodyguard of gray suits and lavender-striped shirts Pearlie and her friend, Miss Evans, walked toward the hotel. The attentive bodyguard confessed itself puzzled.

"Aren't you staying at Pearlie's house?" asked Sid tenderly, when they reached the Burke House. The leading lady glanced up at the windows of the stifling little room that faced west.

"No," answered she, and paused at the foot of the steps to the ladies' entrance. The light from the electric globe over the doorway shone on her hair and sparkled in the folds of her spangled scarf.

"I'm not staying at Pearlie's because my name isn't Ethel Evans. It's Aimee Fox, with a little French accent mark over the double E. I'm leading lady of the 'Second Wife' company and old enough to be—well, your aunty, anyway. We go out at one-thirty to-morrow morning."

IX

That Home-Town Feeling

We all have our ambitions. Mine is to sit in a rocking-chair on the sidewalk at the corner of Clark and Randolph Streets, and watch the crowds go by. South Clark Street is one of the most interesting and cosmopolitan thoroughfares in the world (New Yorkers please sniff). If you are from Paris, France, or Paris, Illinois, and should chance to be in that neighborhood, you will stop at Tony's news stand to buy your home-town paper. Don't mistake the nature of this story. There is nothing of the shivering-newsboy-waif about Tony. He has the voice of a fog-horn, the purple-striped shirt of a sport, the diamond scarf-pin of a racetrack tout, and the savoir faire of the gutter-bred. You'd never pick him for a newsboy if it weren't for his chapped hands and the eternal cold-sore on the upper left corner of his mouth.

It is a fascinating thing, Tony's stand. A high wooden structure rising tier on tier, containing papers from every corner of the world. I'll defy you to name a paper that Tony doesn't handle, from Timbuctoo to Tarrytown, from South Bend to South Africa. A paper marked Christiania, Norway, nestles next to a sheet from Kalamazoo, Michigan. You can get the *War Cry, or Le Figaro*. With one hand, Tony will give you the Berlin *Tageblatt,* and with the other the *Times* from Neenah, Wisconsin. Take your choice between the *Bulletin* from Sydney, Australia, or the *Bee* from Omaha.

But perhaps you know South Clark Street. It is honeycombed with good copy—man-size stuff. South Clark Street reminds one of a slatternly woman, brave in silks and velvets on the surface, but ragged and rumpled and none too clean as to nether garments. It begins with a tenement so vile, so filthy, so repulsive, that the municipal authorities deny its very existence. It ends with a brand-new hotel, all red brick, and white tiling, and Louise Quinze furniture, and sour-cream colored marble lobby, and oriental rugs lavishly scattered under the feet of the unappreciative guest from Kansas City. It is a street of signs, is South Clark.

They vary all the way from "Banca Italiana" done in fat, fly-specked letters of gold, to "Sang Yuen" scrawled in Chinese red and black. Spaghetti and chop suey and dairy lunches nestle side by side. Here an electric sign blazons forth the tempting announcement of lunch. Just across the way, delicately suggesting a means of availing one's self of the invitation, is another which announces "Loans." South Clark Street can transform a winter overcoat into hamburger and onions so quickly that the eye can't follow the hand.

Do you gather from this that you are being taken slumming? Not at all. For the passer-by on Clark Street varies as to color, nationality, raiment, finger-nails, and hair-cut according to the locality in which you find him.

At the tenement end the feminine passer-by is apt to be shawled, swarthy, down-at-the-heel, and dragging a dark-eyed, fretting baby in her wake. At the hotel end you will find her blonde of hair, velvet of boot, plumed of head-gear, and prone to have at her heels a white, woolly, pink-eyed dog.

The masculine Clark Streeter? I throw up my hands. Pray remember that South Clark Street embraces the dime lodging house, pawnshop, hotel, theater, chop-suey and railway office district, all within a few blocks. From the sidewalk in front of his groggery, "Bath House John" can see the City Hall. The trim, khaki-garbed enlistment officer rubs elbows with the lodging house bum. The masculine Clark Streeter may be of the kind that begs a dime for a bed, or he may loll in manicured luxury at the marble-lined hotel. South Clark Street is so splendidly indifferent.

Copy-hunting, I approached Tony with hope in my heart, a smile on my lips, and a nickel in my hand.

"Philadelphia—er—*Inquirer*?" I asked, those being the city and paper which fire my imagination least.

Tony whipped it out, dexterously.

I looked at his keen blue eye, his lean brown face, and his punishing jaw, and I knew that no airy persiflage would deceive him. Boldly I waded in.

"I write for the magazines," said I.

"Do they know it?" grinned Tony.

"Just beginning to be faintly aware. Your stand looks like a story to me. Tell me, does one ever come your way? For instance, don't they come here asking for their home-town paper—sobs in their voice—grasp the sheet with trembling hands—type swims in a misty haze before their eyes—turn aside to brush away a tear—all that kind of stuff, you know?"

Tony's grin threatened his cold-sore. You can't stand on the corner of Clark and Randolph all those years without getting wise to everything there is.

"I'm on," said he, "but I'm afraid I can't accommodate, girlie. I guess my ear ain't attuned to that sob stuff. What's that? Yessir. Nossir, fifteen cents. Well, I can't help that; fifteen's the reg'lar price of foreign papers. Thanks. There, did you see that? I bet that gink give up fifteen of his last two bits to get that paper. O, well, sometimes they look happy, and then again sometimes they—Yes'm. Mississippi? Five cents. Los Vegas *Optic right here*. Hey there! You're forgettin' your change!—an' then again sometimes they look all to the doleful. Say, stick around. Maybe somebody'll start something. You can't never tell."

And then this happened.

A man approached Tony's news stand from the north, and a woman approached Tony's news stand from the south. They brought my story with them.

The woman reeked of the city. I hope you know what I mean. She bore the stamp, and seal, and imprint of it. It had ground its heel down on her face. At the front of her coat she wore a huge bunch of violets, with a fleshy tuberose rising from its center. Her furs were voluminous. Her hat was hidden beneath the cascades of a green willow plume. A green willow plume would make Edna May look sophisticated. She walked with that humping hip movement which city women acquire. She carried a jangling handful of useless gold trinkets. Her heels were too high, and her hair too yellow, and her lips too red, and her nose too white, and her cheeks too pink. Everything about her was "too," from the black stitching on her white gloves to the buckle of brilliants in her hat. The city had her, body and soul, and had fashioned her in its metallic cast. You would have sworn that she had never seen flowers growing in a field.

Said she to Tony:

"Got a Kewaskum *Courier*?"

As she said it the man stopped at the stand and put his question. To present this thing properly I ought to be able to describe them both at the same time, like a juggler keeping two balls in the air at once. Kindly carry the lady in your mind's eye. The man was tall and rawboned, with very white teeth, very blue eyes and an open-faced collar that allowed full play to an objectionably apparent Adam's apple. His hair and mustache were sandy, his gait loping. His manner, clothes, and complexion breathed of Waco, Texas (or is it Arizona?).

Said he to Tony:

"Let me have the London *Times*."

Well, there you are. I turned an accusing eye on Tony.

"And you said no stories came your way," I murmured, reproachfully.

"Help yourself," said Tony.

The blonde lady grasped the Kewaskum *Courier*. Her green plume appeared to be unduly agitated as she searched its columns. The sheet rattled. There was no breeze. The hands in the too-black stitched gloves were trembling.

I turned from her to the man just in time to see the Adam's apple leaping about unpleasantly and convulsively. Whereupon I jumped to two conclusions.

Conclusion one: Any woman whose hands can tremble over the Kewaskum *Courier* is homesick.

Conclusion two: Any man, any part of whose anatomy can become convulsed over the London *Times* is homesick.

She looked up from her *Courier*. He glanced away from his *Times*. As the novelists have it, their eyes met. And there, in each pair of eyes, there swam that misty haze about which I had so earnestly consulted Tony. The Green Plume took an involuntary step forward. The Adam's Apple did the same. They spoke simultaneously.

"They're going to pave Main Street," said the Green Plume, "and Mrs. Wilcox, that was Jeri Meyers, has got another baby girl, and the ladies of the First M. E. made seven dollars and sixty-nine cents on their needlework bazaar and missionary tea. I ain't been home in eleven years."

"Hallem is trying for Parliament in Westchester and the King is back at Windsor. My mother wears a lace cap down to breakfast, and the place is famous for its tapestries and yew trees and family ghost. I haven't been home in twelve years."

The great, soft light of fellow feeling and sympathy glowed in the eyes of each. The Green Plume took still another step forward and laid her hand on his arm (as is the way of Green Plumes the world over).

"Why don't you go, kid?" she inquired, softly.

Adam's Apple gnawed at his mustache end. "I'm the black sheep. Why don't you?"

The blonde lady looked down at her glove tips. Her lower lip was caught between her teeth.

"What's the feminine for black sheep? I'm that. Anyway, I'd be afraid to go home for fear it would be too much of a shock for them when they saw my hair. They wasn't in on the intermediate stages when it was chestnut, auburn, Titian, gold, and orange colored. I want to spare their feelings. The last time they saw me it was just plain brown. Where I come from a woman who dyes her hair when it is beginning to turn gray is considered as good as lost. Funny, ain't it? And yet I remember the minister's wife used to wear false teeth—the kind that clicks. But hair is different."

"Dear lady," said the blue-eyed man, "it would make no difference to your own people. I know they would be happy to see you, hair and all. One's own people—"

"My folks? That's just it. If the Prodigal Son had been a daughter they'd probably have handed her one of her sister's mother hubbards, and put her to work washing dishes in the kitchen. You see, after Ma died my brother married, and I went to live with him and Lil. I was an ugly little mug, and it looked all to the Cinderella for me, with the coach, and four, and prince left out. Lil was the village beauty when my brother married her, and she kind of got into the habit of leaving the heavy role to me, and confining herself to thinking parts. One day I took twenty dollars and came to the city. Oh, I paid it back long ago, but I've never been home since. But say, do you know every time I get near a news stand like this I grab the home-town paper. I'll bet I've kept track every time my sister-in-law's sewing circle has met for the last ten years, and the spring the paper said they built a new porch I was just dying to write and ask 'em what they did with the Virginia creeper that used to cover the whole front and sides of the old porch."

"Look here," said the man, very abruptly, "if it's money you need, why—"

"Me! Do I look like a touch? Now you—"

"Finest stock farm and ranch in seven counties. I come to Chicago once a year to sell. I've got just thirteen thousand nestling next to my left floating rib this minute." The eyes of the woman with the green plume narrowed down to two glittering slits. A new look came into her face—a look that matched her hat, and heels and gloves and complexion and hair.

91

"Thirteen thousand! Thirteen thous— Say, isn't it chilly on this corner, h'm? I know a kind of a restaurant just around the corner where—"

"It's no use," said the sandy-haired man, gently. "And I wouldn't have said that, if I were you. I was going back to-day on the 5:25, but I'm sick of it all. So are you, or you wouldn't have said what you just said. Listen. Let's go back home, you and I. The sight of a Navajo blanket nauseates me. The thought of those prairies makes my eyes ache. I know that if I have to eat one more meal cooked by that Chink of mine I'll hang him by his own pigtail. Those rangy western ponies aren't horseflesh, fit for a man to ride. Why, back home our stables were— Look here. I want to see a silver tea-service, with a coat-of-arms on it. I want to dress for dinner, and take in a girl with a white gown and smooth white shoulders. My sister clips roses in the morning, before breakfast, in a pink ruffled dress and garden gloves. Would you believe that, here, on Clark Street, with a whiskey sign overhead, and the stock-yard smells undernose? O, hell! I'm going home."

"Home?" repeated the blonde lady. "Home?" The sagging lines about her flaccid chin took on a new look of firmness and resolve. The light of determination glowed in her eyes.

"I'll beat you to it," she said. "I'm going home, too. I'll be there to-morrow. I'm dead sick of this. Who cares whether I live or die? It's just one darned round of grease paint, and sky blue tights, and new boarding houses and humping over to the theater every night, going on, and humping back to the room again. I want to wash up some supper dishes with egg on 'em, and set some yeast for bread, and pop a dishpan full of corn, and put a shawl over my head and run over to Millie Krause's to get her kimono sleeve pattern. I'm sour on this dirt and noise. I want to spend the rest of my life in a place so that when I die they'll put a column in the paper, with a verse at the top, and all the neighbors'll come in and help bake up. Here—why, here I'd just be two lines on the want ad page, with fifty cents extra for 'Kewaskum paper please copy.'"

The man held out his hand. "Good-bye," he said, "and please excuse me if I say God bless you. I've never really wanted to say it before, so it's quite extraordinary. My name's Guy Peel."

The white glove, with its too-conspicuous black stitching, disappeared within his palm.

"Mine's Mercedes Meron, late of the Morning Glory Burlesquers, but from now on Sadie Hayes, of Kewaskum, Wisconsin. Good-bye and—well—God bless you, too. Say, I hope you don't think I'm in the habit of talking to strange gents like this."

"I am quite sure you are not," said Guy Peel, very gravely, and bowed slightly before he went south on Clark Street, and she went north.

Dear Reader, will you take my hand while I assist you to make a one year's leap. Whoop-la! There you are.

A man and a woman approached Tony's news stand. You are quite right. But her willow plume was purple this time. A purple willow plume would make Mario Doro look sophisticated. The man was sandy-haired, raw-boned, with a loping gait, very blue eyes, very white teeth, and an objectionably apparent Adam's apple. He came from the north, and she from the south.

In story books, and on the stage, when two people meet unexpectedly after a long separation they always stop short, bring one hand up to their breast, and say: "You!" Sometimes, especially in the case where the heroine chances on the villain, they say, simultaneously: "You! Here!" I have seen people reunited under surprising circumstances, but they never said, "You!" They said something quite unmelodramatic, and commonplace, such as: "Well, look who's here!" or, "My land! If it ain't Ed! How's Ed?"

So it was that the Purple Willow Plume and the Adam's Apple stopped, shook hands, and viewed one another while the Plume said, "I kind of thought I'd bump into you. Felt it in my bones." And the Adam's Apple said:

"Then you're not living in Kewaskum—er—Wisconsin?"

"Not any more," responded she, briskly. "How do you happen to be straying away from the tapestries, and the yew trees and the ghost, and the pink roses, and the garden gloves, and the silver tea-service with the coat-of-arms on it?"

A slow, grim smile overspread the features of the man. "You tell yours first," he said.

"Well," began she, "in the first place, my name's Mercedes Meron, of the Morning Glory Burlesquers, formerly Sadie Hayes of Kewaskum, Wisconsin. I went home next day, like I said I would. Say, Mr. Peel (you said Peel, didn't you? Guy Peel. Nice, neat name), to this day, when I eat lobster late at night, and have dreams, it's always about that visit home."

"How long did you stay?"

"I'm coming to that. Or maybe you can figure it out yourself when I tell you I've been back eleven months. I wired the folks I was coming, and then I came before they had a chance to answer. When the train reached Kewaskum I stepped off into the arms of a dowd in a home-made-made-over-year-before-last suit, and a hat that would have been funny if it hadn't been so pathetic. I grabbed her by the shoulders, and I held her off, and looked—looked at the wrinkles, and the sallow complexion, and the coat with the sleeves in wrong, and the mashed hat (I told you Lil used to be the village peach, didn't I?) and I says:

"'For Gawd's sakes, Lil, does your husband beat you?'

"'Steve!' she shrieks, 'beat me! You must be crazy!'

"'Well, if he don't, he ought to. Those clothes are grounds for divorce,' I says.

"Mr. Guy Peel, it took me just four weeks to get wise to the fact that the way to cure homesickness is to go home. I spent those four weeks trying to revolutionize my sister-in-law's house, dress, kids, husband, wall paper and parlor carpet. I took all the doilies from under the ornaments and spoke my mind on the subject of the hand-painted lamp, and Lil hates me for it yet, and will to her dying day. I fitted three dresses for her, and made her get some corsets that she'll never wear. They have roast pork for dinner on Sundays, and they never go to the theater, and they like bread pudding, and they're happy. I wasn't. They treated me fine, and it was home, all right, but not my home. It was the same, but I was different. Eleven years away from anything makes it shrink, if you know what I mean. I guess maybe you do. I remember that I used to think that the Grand View Hotel was a regular little oriental palace that was almost too luxurious to be respectable, and that the traveling men who stopped there were gods, and just to prance past the hotel after supper had the Atlantic City board walk looking like a back alley on a rainy night. Well, everything had sort of shriveled up just like that. The popcorn gave me indigestion, and I burned the skin off my nose popping it. Kneading bread gave me the backache, and the blamed stuff wouldn't raise right. I got so I was crazy to hear the roar of an L train, and the sound of a crossing policeman's whistle. I got to thinking how Michigan Avenue looks, downtown, with the lights shining down on the asphalt, and all those people eating in the swell hotels, and the autos, and the theater crowds and the windows, and—well, I'm back. Glad I went? You said it. Because it made me so darned glad to get back. I've found out one thing, and it's a great little lesson when you get it learned.

Most of us are where we are because we belong there, and if we didn't, we wouldn't be. Say, that does sound mixed, don't it? But it's straight. Now you tell yours."

"I think you've said it all," began Guy Peel. "It's queer, isn't it, how twelve years of America will spoil one for afternoon tea, and yew trees, and tapestries, and lace caps, and roses. The mater was glad to see me, but she said I smelled woolly. They think a Navajo blanket is a thing the Indians wear on the war path, and they don't know whether Texas is a state, or a mineral water. It was slow—slow. About the time they were taking afternoon tea, I'd be reckoning how the boys would be rounding up the cattle for the night, and about the time we'd sit down to dinner something seemed to whisk the dinner table, and the flowers, and the men and women in evening clothes right out of sight, like magic, and I could see the boys stretched out in front of the bunk house after their supper of bacon, and beans, and biscuit, and coffee. They'd be smoking their pipes that smelled to Heaven, and further, and Wing would be squealing one of his creepy old Chink songs out in the kitchen, and the sky would be—say, Miss Meron, did you ever see the night sky, out West? Purple, you know, and soft as soap-suds, and so near that you want to reach up and touch it with your hand. Toward the end my mother used to take me off in a corner and tell me that I hadn't spoken a word to the little girl that I had taken in to dinner, and that if I couldn't forget my uncouth western ways for an hour or two, at least, perhaps I'd better not try to mingle with civilized people. I discovered that home isn't always the place where you were born and bred. Home is the place where your everyday clothes are, and where somebody, or something needs you. They didn't need me over there in England. Lord no! I was sick for the sight of a Navajo blanket. My shack's glowing with them. And my books needed me, and the boys, and the critters, and Kate."

"Kate?" repeated Miss Meron, quickly.

"Kate's my horse. I'm going back on the 5:25 to-night. This is my regular trip, you know. I came around here to buy a paper, because it has become a habit. And then, too, I sort of felt—well, something told me that you—"

"You're a nice boy," said Miss Meron. "By the way, did I tell you that I married the manager of the show the week after I got back? We go to Bloomington to-night, and then we jump to St. Paul. I came around here just as usual, because—well—because—"

Tony's gift for remembering faces and facts amounts to genius.

With two deft movements he whisked two papers from among the many in the rack, and held them out.

"Kewaskum *Courier*?" he suggested.

"Nix," said Mercedes Meron, "I'll take a Chicago *Scream*."

"London *Times*?" said Tony.

"No," replied Guy Peel. "Give me the *San Antonio Express*."

X

The Homely Heroine

Millie Whitcomb, of the fancy goods and notions, beckoned me with her finger. I had been standing at Kate O'Malley's counter, pretending to admire her new basket-weave suitings, but in reality reveling in her droll account of how, in the train coming up from Chicago, Mrs. Judge Porterfield had worn the negro porter's coat over her chilly shoulders in mistake for her husband's. Kate O'Malley can tell a funny story in a way to make the after-dinner pleasantries of a Washington diplomat sound like the clumsy jests told around the village grocery stove.

"I wanted to tell you that I read that last story of yours," said Millie, sociably, when I had strolled over to her counter, "and I liked it, all but the heroine. She had an 'adorable throat' and hair that 'waved away from her white brow,' and eyes that 'now were blue and now gray.' Say, why don't you write a story about an ugly girl?"

"My land!" protested I. "It's bad enough trying to make them accept my stories as it is. That last heroine was a raving beauty, but she came back eleven times before the editor of *Blakely's* succumbed to her charms."

Millie's fingers were busy straightening the contents of a tray of combs and imitation jet barrettes. Millie's fingers were not intended for that task. They are slender, tapering fingers, pink-tipped and sensitive.

"I should think," mused she, rubbing a cloudy piece of jet with a bit of soft cloth, "that they'd welcome a homely one with relief. These goddesses are so cloying."

Millie Whitcomb's black hair is touched with soft mists of gray, and she wears lavender shirtwaists and white stocks edged with lavender. There is a Colonial air about her that has nothing to do with celluloid combs and imitation jet barrettes. It breathes of dim old rooms, rich with the tones of mahogany and old brass, and Millie in the midst of it, gray-gowned, a soft white fichu crossed upon her breast.

In our town the clerks are not the pert and gum-chewing young persons that story-writers are wont to describe. The girls at Bascom's are institutions. They know us all by our first names, and our lives are as an open book to them. Kate O'Malley, who has been at Bascom's for so many years that she is rumored to have stock in the company, may be said to govern the fashions of our town. She is wont to say, when we express a fancy for gray as the color of our new spring suit:

"Oh, now, Nellie, don't get gray again. You had it year before last, and don't you think it was just the least leetle bit trying? Let me show you that green that came in yesterday. I said the minute I clapped my eyes on it that it was just the color for you, with your brown hair and all."

And we end by deciding on the green.

The girls at Bascom's are not gossips—they are too busy for that— but they may be said to be delightfully well informed. How could they be otherwise when we go to Bascom's for our wedding dresses and party favors and baby flannels? There is news at Bascom's that our daily paper never hears of, and wouldn't dare print if it did.

So when Millie Whitcomb, of the fancy goods and notions, expressed her hunger for a homely heroine, I did not resent the suggestion. On the contrary, it sent me home in thoughtful mood, for Millie Whitcomb has acquired a knowledge of human nature in the dispensing of her fancy goods and notions. It set me casting about for a really homely heroine.

There never has been a really ugly heroine in fiction. Authors have started bravely out to write of an unlovely woman, but they never have had the courage to allow her to remain plain. On Page 237 she puts on a black lace dress and red roses, and the combination brings out unexpected tawny lights in her hair, and olive tints in her cheeks, and there she is, the same old beautiful heroine. Even in the "Duchess" books one finds the simple Irish girl, on donning a green corduroy gown cut square at the neck, transformed into a wild-rose beauty, at sight of whom a ballroom is hushed into admiring awe. There's the case of Jane Eyre, too. She is constantly described as plain and mouse-like, but there are covert hints as to her gray eyes and slender figure and clear skin, and we have a sneaking notion that she wasn't such a fright after all.

Therefore, when I tell you that I am choosing Pearlie Schultz as my leading lady you are to understand that she is ugly, not only when the story opens, but to the bitter end. In the first place, Pearlie is fat. Not plump, or rounded, or dimpled, or deliciously curved, but FAT. She bulges in all the wrong places, including her chin. (Sister, who has a way of snooping over my desk in my absence, says that I may as well drop this now, because nobody would ever read it, anyway, least of all any sane editor. I protest when I discover that Sis has been over my papers. It bothers me. But she says you have to do these things when you have a genius in the house, and cites the case of Kipling's "Recessional," which was rescued from the depths of his wastebasket by his wife.)

Pearlie Schultz used to sit on the front porch summer evenings and watch the couples stroll by, and weep in her heart. A fat girl with a fat girl's soul is a comedy. But a fat girl with a thin girl's soul is a tragedy. Pearlie, in spite of her two hundred pounds, had the soul of a willow wand.

The walk in front of Pearlie's house was guarded by a row of big trees that cast kindly shadows. The strolling couples used to step gratefully into the embrace of these shadows, and from them into other embraces. Pearlie, sitting on the porch, could see them dimly, although they could not see her. She could not help remarking that these strolling couples were strangely lacking in sprightly conversation. Their remarks were but fragmentary, disjointed affairs, spoken in low tones with a queer, tremulous note in them. When they reached the deepest, blackest, kindliest shadow, which fell just before the end of the row of trees, the strolling couples almost always stopped, and then there came a quick movement, and a little smothered cry from the girl, and then a sound, and then a silence. Pearlie, sitting alone on the porch in the dark, listened to these things and blushed furiously. Pearlie had never strolled into the kindly shadows with a little beating of the heart, and she had never been surprised with a quick arm about her and eager lips pressed warmly against her own.

In the daytime Pearlie worked as public stenographer at the Burke Hotel. She rose at seven in the morning, and rolled for fifteen minutes, and lay on her back and elevated her heels in the air, and stood stiff-kneed while she touched the floor with her finger tips one hundred times, and went without her breakfast. At the end of each month she usually found that she weighed three pounds more than she had the month before.

The folks at home never joked with Pearlie about her weight. Even one's family has some respect for a life sorrow. Whenever Pearlie asked that inevitable question of the fat woman: "Am I as fat as she is?" her mother always answered: "You! Well, I should hope not! You're looking real peaked lately, Pearlie. And your blue skirt just ripples in the back, it's getting so big for you."

Of such blessed stuff are mothers made.

But if the gods had denied Pearlie all charms of face or form, they had been decent enough to bestow on her one gift. Pearlie could cook like an angel; no, better than an angel, for no angel could be a really clever cook and wear those flowing kimono-like sleeves. They'd get into the soup. Pearlie could take a piece of rump and some suet and an onion and a cup or so of water, and evolve a pot roast that you could cut with a fork. She could turn out a surprisingly good cake with surprisingly few eggs, all covered with white icing, and bearing cunning little jelly figures on its snowy bosom. She could beat up biscuits that fell apart at the lightest pressure, revealing little pools of golden butter within. Oh, Pearlie could cook!

On week days Pearlie rattled the typewriter keys, but on Sundays she shooed her mother out of the kitchen. Her mother went, protesting faintly:

"Now, Pearlie, don't fuss so for dinner. You ought to get your rest on Sunday instead of stewing over a hot stove all morning."

"Hot fiddlesticks, Ma," Pearlie would say, cheerily. "It ain't hot, because it's a gas stove. And I'll only get fat if I sit around. You put on your black-and-white and go to church. Call me when you've got as far as your corsets, and I'll puff your hair for you in the back."

In her capacity of public stenographer at the Burke Hotel, it was Pearlie's duty to take letters dictated by traveling men and beginning: "Yours of the 10th at hand. In reply would say...." or: "Enclosed please find, etc." As clinching proof of her plainness it may be stated that none of the traveling men, not even Max Baum, who was so fresh that the girl at the cigar counter actually had to squelch him, ever called Pearlie "baby doll," or tried to make a date with her. Not that Pearlie would ever have allowed them to. But she never had had to reprove them. During pauses in dictation she had a way of peering near-sightedly over her glasses at the dapper, well-dressed traveling salesman who was rolling off the items on his sale bill. That is a trick which would make the prettiest kind of a girl look owlish. On the night that Sam Miller strolled up to talk to her, Pearlie was working late. She had promised to get out a long and intricate bill for Max Baum, who travels for Kuhn and Klingman, so that he might take the nine o'clock evening train. The irrepressible Max had departed with much eclat and clatter, and Pearlie was preparing to go home when Sam approached her.

Sam had just come in from the Gayety Theater across the street, whither he had gone in a vain search for amusement after supper. He had come away in disgust. A soiled soubrette with orange-colored hair and baby socks had swept her practiced eye over the audience, and, attracted by Sam's good-looking blond head in the second row, had selected him as the target of her song. She had run up to the extreme edge of the footlights at the risk of teetering over, and had informed Sam through the medium of song—to the huge delight of the audience, and to Sam's red-faced discomfiture—that she liked his smile, and he was just her style, and just as cute as he could be, and just the boy for her. On reaching the chorus she had whipped out a small, round mirror and, assisted by the calcium-light man in the rear, had thrown a wretched little spotlight on Sam's head.

Ordinarily, Sam would not have minded it. But that evening, in the vest pocket just over the place where he supposed his heart to be reposed his girl's daily letter. They were to be married on Sam's return to New York from his first long trip. In the letter near his heart she had written prettily and seriously about traveling men, and traveling men's wives, and her little code for both. The fragrant, girlish, grave little letter had caused Sam to sour on the efforts of the soiled soubrette.

As soon as possible he had fled up the aisle and across the street to the hotel writing-room. There he had spied Pearlie's good-humored, homely face, and its contrast with the silly, red and-white countenance of the unlaundered soubrette had attracted his homesick heart.

Pearlie had taken some letters from him earlier in the day. Now, in his hunger for companionship, he strolled up to her desk, just as she was putting her typewriter to bed.

"Gee, this is a lonesome town!" said Sam, smiling down at her.

Pearlie glanced up at him, over her glasses. "I guess you must be from New York," she said. "I've heard a real New Yorker can get bored in Paris. In New York the sky is bluer, and the grass is greener, and the girls are prettier, and the steaks are thicker, and the buildings are higher, and the streets are wider, and the air is finer, than the sky, or the grass, or the girls, or the steaks, or the air of any place else in the world. Ain't they?"

"Oh, now," protested Sam, "quit kiddin' me! You'd be lonesome for the little old town, too, if you'd been born and dragged up in it, and hadn't seen it for four months."

"New to the road, aren't you?" asked Pearlie.

Sam blushed a little. "How did you know?"

"Well, you generally can tell. They don't know what to do with themselves evenings, and they look rebellious when they go into the dining-room. The old-timers just look resigned."

"You've picked up a thing or two around here, haven't you? I wonder if the time will ever come when I'll look resigned to a hotel dinner, after four months of 'em. Why, girl, I've got so I just eat the things that are covered up—like baked potatoes in the shell, and soft boiled eggs, and baked apples, and oranges that I can peel, and nuts."

"Why, you poor kid," breathed Pearlie, her pale eyes fixed on him in motherly pity. "You oughtn't to do that. You'll get so thin your girl won't know you."

Sam looked up quickly. "How in thunderation did you know—?"

Pearlie was pinning on her hat, and she spoke succinctly, her hatpins between her teeth: "You've been here two days now, and I notice you dictate all your letters except the longest one, and you write that one off in a corner of the writing-room all by yourself, with your cigar just glowing like a live coal, and you squint up through the smoke, and grin to yourself."

"Say, would you mind if I walked home with you?" asked Sam.

If Pearlie was surprised, she was woman enough not to show it. She picked up her gloves and hand bag, locked her drawer with a click, and smiled her acquiescence. And when Pearlie smiled she was awful.

It was a glorious evening in the early summer, moonless, velvety, and warm. As they strolled homeward, Sam told her all about the Girl, as is the way of traveling men the world over. He told her about the tiny apartment they had taken, and how he would be on the road only a couple of years more, as this was just a try-out that the firm always insisted on. And they stopped under an arc light while Sam showed her the picture in his watch, as is also the way of traveling men since time immemorial.

Pearlie made an excellent listener. He was so boyish, and so much in love, and so pathetically eager to make good with the firm, and so happy to have some one in whom to confide.

"But it's a dog's life, after all," reflected Sam, again after the fashion of all traveling men. "Any fellow on the road earns his salary these days, you bet. I used to think it was all getting up when you felt like it, and sitting in the big front window of the hotel, smoking a cigar and watching the pretty girls go by. I wasn't wise to the packing, and the unpacking, and the rotten train service, and the grouchy customers, and the canceled bills, and the grub."

Pearlie nodded understandingly. "A man told me once that twice a week regularly he dreamed of the way his wife cooked noodle-soup."

"My folks are German," explained Sam. "And my mother—can she cook! Well, I just don't seem able to get her potato pancakes out of my mind. And her roast beef tasted and looked like roast beef, and not like a wet red flannel rag."

At this moment Pearlie was seized with a brilliant idea. "To-morrow's Sunday. You're going to Sunday here, aren't you? Come over and eat your dinner with us. If you have forgotten the taste of real food, I can give you a dinner that'll jog your memory."

"Oh, really," protested Sam. "You're awfully good, but I couldn't think of it. I—"

"You needn't be afraid. I'm not letting you in for anything. I may be homelier than an English suffragette, and I know my lines are all bumps, but there's one thing you can't take away from me, and that's my cooking hand. I can cook, boy, in a way to make your mother's Sunday dinner, with company expected, look like Mrs. Newlywed's first attempt at 'riz' biscuits. And I don't mean any disrespect to your mother when I say it. I'm going to have noodle-soup, and fried chicken, and hot biscuits, and creamed beans from our own garden, and strawberry shortcake with real—"

"Hush!" shouted Sam. "If I ain't there, you'll know that I passed away during the night, and you can telephone the clerk to break in my door."

The Grim Reaper spared him, and Sam came, and was introduced to the family, and ate. He put himself in a class with Dr. Johnson, and Ben Brust, and Gargantua, only that his table manners were better. He almost forgot to talk during the soup, and he came back three times for chicken, and by the time the strawberry shortcake was half consumed he was looking at Pearlie with a sort of awe in his eyes.

That night he came over to say good-bye before taking his train out for Ishpeming. He and Pearlie strolled down as far as the park and back again.

"I didn't eat any supper," said Sam. "It would have been sacrilege, after that dinner of yours. Honestly, I don't know how to thank you, being so good to a stranger like me. When I come back next trip, I expect to have the Kid with me, and I want her to meet you, by George!

She's a winner and a pippin, but she wouldn't know whether a porterhouse was stewed or frapped. I'll tell her about you, you bet. In the meantime, if there's anything I can do for you, I'm yours to command."

Pearlie turned to him suddenly. "You see that clump of thick shadows ahead of us, where those big trees stand in front of our house?"

"Sure," replied Sam.

"Well, when we step into that deepest, blackest shadow, right in front of our porch, I want you to reach up, and put your arm around me and kiss me on the mouth, just once. And when you get back to New York you can tell your girl I asked you to."

There broke from him a little involuntary exclamation. It might have been of pity, and it might have been of surprise. It had in it something of both, but nothing of mirth. And as they stepped into the depths of the soft black shadows he took off his smart straw sailor, which was so different from the sailors that the boys in our town wear. And there was in the gesture something of reverence.

Millie Whitcomb didn't like the story of the homely heroine, after all. She says that a steady diet of such literary fare would give her blue indigestion. Also she objects on the ground that no one got married—that is, the heroine didn't. And she says that a heroine who does not get married isn't a heroine at all. She thinks she prefers the pink-cheeked goddess kind, in the end.

XI

Sun Dried

There come those times in the life of every woman when she feels that she must wash her hair at once. And then she does it. The feeling may come upon her suddenly, without warning, at any hour of the day or night; or its approach may be slow and insidious, so that the victim does not at first realize what it is that fills her with that sensation of unrest. But once in the clutches of the idea she knows no happiness, no peace, until she has donned a kimono, gathered up two bath towels, a spray, and the green soap, and she breathes again only when, head dripping, she makes for the back yard, the sitting-room radiator, or the side porch (depending on her place of residence, and the time of year).

Mary Louise was seized with the feeling at ten o'clock on a joyous June morning. She tried to fight it off because she had got to that stage in the construction of her story where her hero was beginning to talk and act a little more like a real live man, and a little less like a clothing store dummy. (By the way, they don't seem to be using those pink-and-white, black-mustachioed figures any more. Another good simile gone.)

Mary Louise had been battling with that hero for a week. He wouldn't make love to the heroine. In vain had Mary Louise striven to instill red blood into his watery veins. He and the beauteous heroine were as far apart as they had been on Page One of the typewritten manuscript. Mary Louise was developing nerves over him. She had bitten her finger nails, and twisted her hair into corkscrews over him. She had risen every morning at the chaste hour of seven, breakfasted hurriedly, tidied the tiny two-room apartment, and sat down in the unromantic morning light to wrestle with her stick of a hero. She had made her heroine a creature of grace, wit, and loveliness, but thus far the hero had not once clasped her to him fiercely, or pressed his lips to her hair, her eyes, her cheeks. Nay (as the story-writers would put it), he hadn't even devoured her with his gaze.

This morning, however, he had begun to show some signs of life. He was developing possibilities. Whereupon, at this critical stage in the story-writing game, the hair-washing mania seized Mary Louise. She tried to dismiss the idea. She pushed it out of her mind, and slammed the door. It only popped in again. Her fingers wandered to her hair. Her eyes wandered to the June sunshine outside. The hero was left poised, arms outstretched, and unquenchable love-light burning in his eyes, while Mary Louise mused, thus:

"It certainly feels sticky. It's been six weeks, at least. And I could sit here—by the window—in the sun—and dry it—"

With a jerk she brought her straying fingers away from her hair, and her wandering eyes away from the sunshine, and her runaway thoughts back to the typewritten page. For three minutes the snap of the little disks crackled through the stillness of the tiny apartment. Then, suddenly, as though succumbing to an irresistible force, Mary Louise rose, walked across the room (a matter of six steps), removing hairpins as she went, and shoved aside the screen which hid the stationary wash-bowl by day.

Mary Louise turned on a faucet and held her finger under it, while an agonized expression of doubt and suspense overspread her features. Slowly the look of suspense gave way to a smile of beatific content. A sigh—deep, soul-filling, satisfied—welled up from Mary Louise's breast. The water was hot.

Half an hour later, head swathed turban fashion in a towel, Mary Louise strolled over to the window. Then she stopped, aghast. In that half hour the sun had slipped just around the corner, and was now beating brightly and uselessly against the brick wall a few inches away. Slowly Mary Louise unwound the towel, bent double in the contortionistic attitude that women assume on such occasions, and watched with melancholy eyes while the drops trickled down to the ends of her hair, and fell, unsunned, to the floor.

"If only," thought Mary Louise, bitterly, "there was such a thing as a back yard in this city—a back yard where I could squat on the grass, in the sunshine and the breeze— Maybe there is. I'll ask the janitor."

She bound her hair in the turban again, and opened the door. At the far end of the long, dim hallway Charlie, the janitor, was doing something to the floor with a mop and a great deal of sloppy water, whistling the while with a shrill abandon that had announced his presence to Mary Louise.

"Oh, Charlie!" called Mary Louise. "Charlee! Can you come here just a minute?"

"You bet!" answered Charlie, with the accent on the you; and came.

"Charlie, is there a back yard, or something, where the sun is, you know—some nice, grassy place where I can sit, and dry my hair, and let the breezes blow it?"

"Back yard!" grinned Charlie. "I guess you're new to N' York, all right, with ground costin' a million or so a foot. Not much they ain't no back yard, unless you'd give that name to an ash-barrel, and a dump heap or so, and a crop of tin cans. I wouldn't invite a goat to set in it."

Disappointment curved Mary Louise's mouth. It was a lovely enough mouth at any time, but when it curved in disappointment—well, janitors are but human, after all.

"Tell you what, though," said Charlie. "I'll let you up on the roof. It ain't long on grassy spots up there, but say, breeze! Like a summer resort. On a clear day you can see way over 's far 's Eight' Avenoo. Only for the love of Mike don't blab it to the other women folks in the buildin', or I'll have the whole works of 'em usin' the roof for a general sun, massage, an' beauty parlor. Come on."

"I'll never breathe it to a soul," promised Mary Louise, solemnly. "Oh, wait a minute."

She turned back into her room, appearing again in a moment with something green in her hand.

"What's that?" asked Charlie, suspiciously.

Mary Louise, speeding down the narrow hallway after Charlie, blushed a little. "It—it's parsley," she faltered.

"Parsley!" exploded Charlie. "Well, what the—"

"Well, you see. I'm from the country," explained Mary Louise, "and in the country, at this time of year, when you dry your hair in the back yard, you get the most wonderful scent of green and growing things—not only of flowers, you know, but of the new things just coming up in the vegetable garden, and—and—well, this parsley happens to be the only really gardeny thing I have, so I thought I'd bring it along and sniff it once in a while, and make believe it's the country, up there on the roof."

Half-way up the perilous little flight of stairs that led to the roof, Charlie, the janitor, turned to gaze down at Mary Louise, who was just behind, and keeping fearfully out of the way of Charlie's heels.

"Wimmin," observed Charlie, the janitor, "is nothin' but little girls in long skirts, and their hair done up."

"I know it," giggled Mary Louise, and sprang up on the roof, looking, with her towel-swathed head, like a lady Aladdin leaping from her underground grotto.

The two stood there a moment, looking up at the blue sky, and all about at the June sunshine.

"If you go up high enough," observed Mary Louise, "the sunshine is almost the same as it is in the country, isn't it?"

"I shouldn't wonder," said Charlie, "though Calvary cemetery is about as near's I'll ever get to the country. Say, you can set here on this soap box and let your feet hang down. The last janitor's wife used to hang her washin' up here, I guess. I'll leave this door open, see?"

"You're so kind," smiled Mary Louise.

"Kin you blame me?" retorted the gallant Charles. And vanished.

Mary Louise, perched on the soap box, unwound her turban, draped the damp towel over her shoulders, and shook out the wet masses of her hair. Now the average girl shaking out the wet masses of her hair looks like a drowned rat. But Nature had been kind to Mary Louise. She had given her hair that curled in little ringlets when wet, and that waved in all the right places when dry.

Just now it hung in damp, shining strands on either side of her face, so that she looked most remarkably like one of those oval-faced, great-eyed, red-lipped women that the old Italian artists were so fond of painting.

Below her, blazing in the sun, lay the great stone and iron city. Mary Louise shook out her hair idly, with one hand, sniffed her parsley, shut her eyes, threw back her head, and began to sing, beating time with her heel against the soap box, and forgetting all about the letter that had come that morning, stating that it was not from any lack of merit, etc. She sang, and sniffed her parsley, and waggled her hair in the breeze, and beat time, idly, with the heel of her little boot, when—

"Holy Cats!" exclaimed a man's voice. "What is this, anyway? A Coney Island concession gone wrong?"

Mary Louise's eyes unclosed in a flash, and Mary Louise gazed upon an irate-looking, youngish man, who wore shabby slippers, and no collar with a full dress air.

"I presume that you are the janitor's beautiful daughter," growled the collarless man.

"Well, not precisely," answered Mary Louise, sweetly. "Are you the scrub-lady's stalwart son?"

"Ha!" exploded the man. "But then, all women look alike with their hair down. I ask your pardon, though."

"Not at all," replied Mary Louise. "For that matter, all men look like picked chickens with their collars off."

At that the collarless man, who until now had been standing on the top step that led up to the roof, came slowly forward, stepped languidly over a skylight or two, draped his handkerchief over a convenient chimney and sat down, hugging his long, lean legs to him.

"Nice up here, isn't it?" he remarked.

"It was," said Mary Louise.

"Ha!" exploded he, again. Then, "Where's your mirror?" he demanded.

"Mirror?" echoed Mary Louise.

"Certainly. You have the hair, the comb, the attitude, and the general Lorelei effect. Also your singing lured me to your shores."

"You didn't look lured," retorted Mary Louise. "You looked lurid."

"What's that stuff in your hand?" next demanded he. He really was a most astonishingly rude young man.

"Parsley."

"Parsley!" shouted he, much as Charlie had done. "Well, what the—"

"Back home," elucidated Mary Louise once more, patiently, "after you've washed your hair you dry it in the back yard, sitting on the grass, in the sunshine and the breeze. And the garden smells come to you—the nasturtiums, and the pansies, and the geraniums, you know, and even that clean grass smell, and the pungent vegetable odor, and there are ants, and bees, and butterflies—"

"Go on," urged the young man, eagerly.

"And Mrs. Next Door comes out to hang up a few stockings, and a jabot or so, and a couple of baby dresses that she has just rubbed through, and she calls out to you:

"'Washed your hair?'

"'Yes,' you say. 'It was something awful, and I wanted it nice for Tuesday night. But I suppose I won't be able to do a thing with it.'

"And then Mrs. Next Door stands there a minute on the clothes-reel platform, with the wind whipping her skirts about her, and the fresh smell of the growing things coming to her. And suddenly she says: 'I guess I'll wash mine too, while the baby's asleep.'"

The collarless young man rose from his chimney, picked up his handkerchief, and moved to the chimney just next to Mary Louise's soap box.

"Live here?" he asked, in his impolite way.

"If I did not, do you think that I would choose this as the one spot in all New York in which to dry my hair?"

"When I said, 'Live here,' I didn't mean just that. I meant who are you, and why are you here, and where do you come from, and do you sign your real name to your stuff, or use a nom de plume?"

"Why—how did you know?" gasped Mary Louise.

"Give me five minutes more," grinned the keen-eyed young man, "and I'll tell you what make your typewriter is, and where the last rejection slip came from."

"Oh!" said Mary Louise again. "Then you *are* the scrub-lady's stalwart son, and you've been ransacking my wastebasket."

Quite unheeding, the collarless man went on, "And so you thought you could write, and you came on to New York (you know one doesn't just travel to New York, or ride to it, or come to it; one 'comes on' to New York), and now you're not so sure about the writing, h'm? And back home what did you do?"

"Back home I taught school—and hated it. But I kept on teaching until I'd saved five hundred dollars. Every other school ma'am in the world teaches until she has saved five hundred dollars, and then she packs two suit-cases, and goes to Europe from June until September. But I saved my five hundred for New York. I've been here six months now, and the five hundred has shrunk to almost nothing, and if I don't break into the magazines pretty soon—"

"Then?"

"Then," said Mary Louise, with a quaver in her voice, "I'll have to go back and teach thirty-seven young devils that six times five is thirty, put down the naught and carry six, and that the French are a gay people, fond of dancing and light wines. But I'll scrimp on everything from hairpins to shoes, and back again, including pretty collars, and gloves, and hats, until I've saved up another five hundred, and then I'll try it all over again, because I—can—write."

From the depths of one capacious pocket the inquiring man took a small black pipe, from another a bag of tobacco, from another a match. The long, deft fingers made a brief task of it.

"I didn't ask you," he said, after the first puff, "because I could see that you weren't the fool kind that objects." Then, with amazing suddenness, "Know any of the editors?"

"Know them!" cried Mary Louise. "Know them! If camping on their doorsteps, and haunting the office buildings, and cajoling, and fighting with secretaries and office boys, and assistants and things constitutes knowing them, then we're chums."

"What makes you think you can write?" sneered the thin man.

Mary Louise gathered up her brush, and comb, and towel, and parsley, and jumped off the soap box. She pointed belligerently at her tormentor with the hand that held the brush.

"Being the scrub-lady's stalwart son, you wouldn't understand. But I can write. I sha'n't go under. I'm going to make this town count me in as the four million and oneth. Sometimes I get so tired of being nobody at all, with not even enough cleverness in me to wrest a living from this big city, that I long to stand out at the edge of the curbing, and take off my hat, and wave it, and shout, 'Say, you four million uncaring people, I'm Mary Louise Moss, from Escanaba, Michigan, and I like your town, and I want to stay here. Won't you please pay some slight attention to me. No one knows I'm here except myself, and the rent collector.'"

"And I," put in the rude young man.

"O, you," sneered Mary Louise, equally rude, "you don't count."

The collarless young man in the shabby slippers smiled a curious little twisted smile. "You never can tell," he grinned, "I might." Then, quite suddenly, he stood up, knocked the ash out of his pipe, and came over to Mary Louise, who was preparing to descend the steep little flight of stairs.

"Look here, Mary Louise Moss, from Escanaba, Michigan, you stop trying to write the slop you're writing now. Stop it. Drop the love tales that are like the stuff that everybody else writes. Stop trying to write about New York. You don't know anything about it. Listen. You get back to work, and write about Mrs. Next Door, and the hair-washing, and the vegetable garden, and bees, and the back yard, understand? You write the way you talked to me, and then you send your stuff in to Cecil Reeves."

"Reeves!" mocked Mary Louise. "Cecil Reeves, of *The Earth*? He wouldn't dream of looking at my stuff. And anyway, it really isn't your affair." And began to descend the stairs.

"Well, you know you brought me up here, kicking with your heels, and singing at the top of your voice. I couldn't work. So it's really your fault." Then, just as Mary Louise had almost disappeared down the stairway he put his last astonishing question.

"How often do you wash your hair?" he demanded.

"Well, back home," confessed Mary Louise, "every six weeks or so was enough, but—"

"Not here," put in the rude young man, briskly. "Never. That's all very well for the country, but it won't do in the city. Once a week, at least, and on the roof. Cleanliness demands it."

"But if I'm going back to the country," replied Mary Louise, "it won't be necessary."

"But you're not," calmly said the collarless young man, just as Mary Louise vanished from sight.

Down at the other end of the hallway on Mary Louise's floor Charlie, the janitor, was doing something to the windows now, with a rag, and a pail of water.

"Get it dry?" he called out, sociably.

"Yes, thank you," answered Mary Louise, and turned to enter her own little apartment. Then, hesitatingly, she came back to Charlie's window.

"There—there was a man up there—a very tall, very thin, very rude, very—that is, rather nice youngish oldish man, in slippers, and no collar. I wonder—"

"Oh, him!" snorted Charlie. "He don't show himself onct in a blue moon. None of the other tenants knows he's up there. Has the whole top floor to himself, and shuts himself up there for weeks at a time, writin' books, or some such truck. That guy, he owns the building."

"Owns the building!" said Mary Louise, faintly. "Why he looked—he looked—"

"Sure," grinned Charlie. "That's him. Name's Reeves—Cecil Reeves. Say, ain't that a divil of a name?"

XII

Where the Car Turns at 18th

This will be a homing pigeon story. Though I send it ever so far—though its destination be the office of a home-and-fireside magazine or one of the kind with a French story in the back, it will return to me. After each flight its feathers will be a little more rumpled, its wings more weary, its course more wavering, until, battered, spent, broken, it will flutter to rest in the waste basket.

And yet, though its message may never be delivered, it must be sent, because—well, because—

You know where the car turns at Eighteenth? There you see a glaringly attractive billboard poster. It depicts groups of smiling, white-clad men standing on tropical shores, with waving palms overhead, and a glimpse of blue sea in the distance. The wording beneath the picture runs something like this:

"Young men wanted. An unusual opportunity for travel, education, and advancement. Good pay. No expenses."

When the car turns at Eighteenth, and I see that, I remember Eddie Houghton back home. And when I remember Eddie Houghton I see red.

The day after Eddie Houghton finished high school he went to work. In our town we don't take a job. We accept a position. Our paper had it that "Edwin Houghton had accepted a position as clerk and assistant chemist at the Kunz drugstore, where he would take up his new duties Monday."

His new duties seemed, at first, to consist of opening the store in the morning, sweeping out, and whizzing about town on a bicycle with an unnecessarily insistent bell, delivering prescriptions which had been telephoned for. But by the time the summer had really set in Eddie was installed back of the soda fountain.

There never was anything better looking than Eddie Houghton in his white duck coat. He was one of those misleadingly gold and pink and white men. I say misleadingly because you usually associate pink-and-whiteness with such words as sissy and mollycoddle. Eddie was neither. He had played quarter-back every year from his freshman year, and he could putt the shot and cut classes with the best of 'em. But in that white duck coat with the braiding and frogs he had any musical-comedy, white-flannel tenor lieutenant whose duty it is to march down to the edge of the footlights, snatch out his sword, and warble about his country's flag, looking like a flat-nosed, blue-gummed Igorrote. Kunz's soda water receipts swelled to double their usual size, and the girls' complexions were something awful that summer. I've known Nellie Donovan to take as many as three ice cream sodas and two phosphates a day when Eddie was mixing. He had a way of throwing in a good-natured smile, and an easy flow of conversation with every drink. While indulging in a little airy persiflage the girls had a great little trick of pursing their mouths into rosebud shapes over their soda straws, and casting their eyes upward at Eddie. They all knew the trick, and its value, so that at night Eddie's dreams were haunted by whole rows of rosily pursed lips, and seas of upturned, adoring eyes. Of course we all noticed that on those rare occasions when Josie Morehouse came into Kunz's her glass was heaped higher with ice cream than that of any of the other girls, and that Eddie's usually easy flow of talk was interspersed with certain stammerings and stutterings. But Josie didn't come in often. She had a lot of dignity for a girl of eighteen. Besides, she was taking the teachers' examinations that summer, when the other girls were playing tennis and drinking sodas.

Eddie really hated the soda water end of the business, as every soda clerk in the world does. But he went about it good-naturedly. He really wanted to learn the drug business, but the boss knew he had a drawing card, and insisted that Eddie go right on concocting faerie queens and strawberry sundaes, and nectars and Kunz's specials. One Saturday, when he happened to have on hand an over-supply of bananas that would have spoiled over Sunday, he invented a mess and called it the Eddie Extra, and the girls swarmed on it like flies around a honey pot.

That kind of thing would have spoiled most boys. But Eddie had a sensible mother. On those nights when he used to come home nauseated with dealing out chop suey sundaes and orangeades, and saying that there was no future for a fellow in our dead little hole, his mother would give him something rather special for supper, and set him hoeing and watering the garden.

So Eddie stuck to his job, and waited, and all the time he was saying, with a melting look, to the last silly little girl who was drinking her third soda, "Somebody looks mighty sweet in pink to-day," or while he was doping to-morrow's ball game with one of the boys who dropped in for a cigar, he was thinking of bigger things, and longing for a man-size job.

The man-size job loomed up before Eddie's dazzled eyes when he least expected it. It was at the close of a particularly hot day when it seemed to Eddie that every one in town had had everything from birch beer to peach ice cream. On his way home to supper he stopped at the postoffice with a handful of letters that old man Kunz had given him to mail. His mother had told him that they would have corn out of their own garden for supper that night, and Eddie was in something of a hurry. He and his mother were great pals.

In one corner of the dim little postoffice lobby a man was busily tacking up posters. The whitewashed walls bloomed with them. They were gay, attractive-looking posters, done in red and blue and green, and after Eddie had dumped his mail into the slot, and had called out, "Hello, Jake!" to the stamp clerk, whose back was turned to the window, he strolled idly over to where the man was putting the finishing touches to his work. The man was dressed in a sailor suit of blue, with a picturesque silk scarf knotted at his hairy chest. He went right on tacking posters. They certainly were attractive pictures. Some showed groups of stalwart, immaculately clad young gods lolling indolently on tropical shores, with a splendor of palms overhead, and a sparkling blue sea in the distance. Others depicted a group of white-clad men wading knee-deep in the surf as they laughingly landed a cutter on the sandy beach. There was a particularly fascinating one showing two barefooted young chaps on a wave-swept raft engaged in that delightfully perilous task known as signaling. Another showed the keen-eyed gunners busy about the big guns. Eddie studied them all.

The man finished his task and looked up, quite casually.

"Hello, kid," he said.

"Hello," answered Eddie. Then—"That's some picture gallery you're giving us."

The man in the sailor suit fell back a pace or two and surveyed his work with a critical but satisfied eye.

"Pitchers," he said, "don't do it justice. We've opened a recruiting office here. Looking for young men with brains, and muscle, and ambition. It's a great chance. We don't get to these here little towns much."

He placed a handbill in Eddie's hand. Eddie glanced down at it sheepishly.

"I've heard," he said, "that it's a hard life."

The man in the sailor suit threw back his head and laughed, displaying a great deal of hairy throat and chest. "Hard!" he jeered, and slapped one of the gay-colored posters with the back of his hand. "You see that! Well, it ain't a bit exaggerated. Not a bit. I ought to know. It's the only life for a young man, especially for a guy in a little town. There's no chance here for a bright young man, and if he goes to the city, what does he get? The city's jam full of kids that flock there in the spring and fall, looking for jobs, and thinking the city's sittin' up waitin' for 'em. And where do they land? In the dime lodging houses, that's where. In the navy you see the world, and it don't cost you a cent. A guy is a fool to bury himself alive in a hole like this. You could be seeing the world, traveling by sea from port to port, from country to country, from ocean to ocean, amid ever-changing scenery and climatic conditions, to see and study the habits and conditions of the strange races—"

It rolled off his tongue with fascinating glibness. Eddie glanced at the folder in his hand.

"I always did like the water," he said.

"Sure," agreed the hairy man, heartily. "What young feller don't? I'll tell you what. Come on over to the office with me and I'll show you some real stuff."

"It's my supper time," hesitated Eddie. "I guess I'd better not—"

"Oh, supper," laughed the man. "You come on and have supper with me, kid."

Eddie's pink cheeks went three shades pinker. "Gee! That'd be great. But my mother—that is—she—"

The man in the sailor suit laughed again—a laugh with a sting in it. "A great big feller like you ain't tied to your ma's apron strings are you?"

"Not much I'm not!" retorted Eddie. "I'll telephone her when I get to your hotel, that's what I'll do."

But they were such fascinating things, those new booklets, and the man had such marvelous tales to tell, that Eddie forgot trifles like supper and waiting mothers. There were pictures taken on board ship, showing frolics, and ball games, and minstrel shows and glee clubs, and the men at mess, and each sailor sleeping snug as a bug in his hammock. There were other pictures showing foreign scenes and strange ports. Eddie's tea grew cold, and his apple pie and cheese lay untasted on his plate.

116

"Now me," said the recruiting officer, "I'm a married man. But my wife, she wouldn't have it no other way. No, sir! She'll be in the navy herself, I'll bet, when women vote. Why, before I joined the navy I didn't know whether Guam was a vegetable or an island, and Culebra wasn't in my geography. Now? Why, now I'm as much at home in Porto Rico as I am in San Francisco. I'm as well acquainted in Valparaiso as I am in Vermont, and I've run around Cairo, Egypt, until I know it better than Cairo, Illinois. It's the only way to see the world. You travel by sea from port to port, from country to country, from ocean to ocean, amid ever-changing scenery and climatic conditions, to see and study the—"

And Eddie forgot that it was Wednesday night, which was the pre-scription clerk's night off; forgot that the boss was awaiting his return that he might go home to his own supper; forgot his mother, and her little treat of green corn out of the garden; forgot everything in the wonder of this man's tales of people and scenes such as he never dreamed could exist outside of a Jack London story. Now and then Eddie interrupted with a "Yes, but—" that grew more and more infrequent, until finally they ceased altogether. Eddie's man-size job had come.

When we heard the news we all dropped in at the drug store to joke with him about it. We had a good deal to say about rolling gaits, and bell-shaped trousers, and anchors and sea serpents tattooed on the arm. One of the boys scored a hit by slapping his dime down on the soda fountain marble and bellowing for rum and salt horse. Some one started to tease the little Morehouse girl about sailors having sweethearts in every port, but when they saw the look in her eyes they changed their mind, and stopped. It's funny how a girl of twenty is a woman, when a man of twenty is a boy.

Eddie dished out the last of his chocolate ice cream sodas and cherry phosphates and root beers, while the girls laughingly begged him to bring them back kimonos from China, and scarves from the Orient, and Eddie promised, laughing, too, but with a far-off, eager look in his eyes.

When the time came for him to go there was quite a little bodyguard of us ready to escort him down to the depot. We picked up two or three more outside O'Rourke's pool room, and a couple more from the benches outside the hotel. Eddie walked ahead with his mother. I have said that Mrs. Houghton was a sensible woman. She was never more so than now. Any other mother would have gone into hysterics and begged the recruiting officer to let her boy off. But she knew better. Still, I think

Eddie felt some uncomfortable pangs when he looked at her set face. On the way to the depot we had to pass the Agassiz School, where Josie Morehouse was substituting second reader for the Wilson girl, who was sick. She was standing in the window as we passed. Eddie took off his cap and waved to her, and she returned the wave as well as she could without having the children see her. That would never have done, seeing that she was the teacher, and substituting at that. But when we turned the corner we noticed that she was still standing at the window and leaning out just a bit, even at the risk of being indiscreet.

When the 10:15 pulled out Eddie stood on the bottom step, with his cap off, looking I can't tell you how boyish, and straight, and clean, and handsome, with his lips parted, and his eyes very bright. The hairy-chested recruiting officer stood just beside him, and suffered by contrast. There was a bedlam of good-byes, and last messages, and good-natured badinage, but Eddie's mother's eyes never left his face until the train disappeared around the curve in the track.

Well, they got a new boy at Kunz's—a sandy-haired youth, with pimples, and no knack at mixing, and we got out of the habit of dropping in there, although those fall months were unusually warm.

It wasn't long before we began to get postcards—pictures of the naval training station, and the gymnasium, and of model camps and of drills, and of Eddie in his uniform. His mother insisted on calling it his sailor suit, as though he were a little boy. One day Josie Morehouse came over to Mrs. Houghton's with a group picture in her hand. She handed it to Eddie's mother without comment. Mrs. Houghton looked at it eagerly, her eye selecting her own boy from the group as unerringly as a mother bird finds her nest in the forest.

"Oh, Eddie's better looking than that!" she cried, with a tremulous little laugh. "How funny those pants make them look, don't they? And his mouth isn't that way, at all. Eddie always had the sweetest mouth, from the time he was a baby. Let's see some of these other boys. Why—why—"

Then she fell silent, scanning those other faces. Presently Josie bent over her and looked too, and the brows of both women knitted in perplexity. They looked for a long, long minute, and the longer they looked the more noticeable became the cluster of fine little wrinkles that had begun to form about Mrs. Houghton's eyes.

When finally they looked up it was to gaze at one another questioningly.

"Those other boys," faltered Eddie's mother, "they—they don't look like Eddie, do they? I mean—"

"No, they don't," agreed Josie. "They look older, and they have such queer-looking eyes, and jaws, and foreheads. But then," she finished, with mock cheerfulness, "you can never tell in those silly Kodak pictures."

Eddie's mother studied the card again, and sighed gently. "I hope," she said, "that Eddie won't get into bad company."

After that our postal cards ceased. I wish that there was some way of telling this story so that the end wouldn't come in the middle. But there is none. In our town we know the news before the paper comes out, and we only read it to verify what we have heard. So that long before the paper came out in the middle of the afternoon we had been horrified by the news of Eddie Houghton's desertion and suicide. We stopped one another on Main Street to talk about it, and recall how boyish and handsome he had looked in his white duck coat, and on that last day just as the 10:15 pulled out. "It don't seem hardly possible, does it?" we demanded of each other.

But when Eddie's mother brought out the letters that had come after our postal cards had ceased, we understood. And when they brought him home, and we saw him for the last time, all those of us who had gone to school with him, and to dances, and sleigh rides, and hayrack parties, and picnics, and when we saw the look on his face—the look of one who, walking in a sunny path has stumbled upon something horrible and unclean—we forgave him his neglect of us, we forgave him desertion, forgave him the taking of his own life, forgave him the look that he had brought into his mother's eyes.

There had never been anything extraordinary about Eddie Houghton. He had had his faults and virtues, and good and bad sides just like other boys of his age. He—oh, I am using too many words, when one slang phrase will express it. Eddie had been just a nice young kid. I think the worst thing he had ever said was "Damn!" perhaps. If he had sworn, it was with clean oaths, calculated to relieve the mind and feelings.

But the men that he shipped with during that year or more—I am sure that he had never dreamed that such men were. He had never stood on the curbing outside a recruiting office on South State Street, in the old levee district, and watched that tragic panorama move by—those nightmare faces, drink-marred, vice-scarred, ruined.

119

I know that he had never seen such faces in all his clean, hard-working young boy's life, spent in our prosperous little country town. I am certain that he had never heard such words as came from the lips of his fellow seamen—great mouth-filling, soul-searing words—words unclean, nauseating, unspeakable, and yet spoken.

I don't say that Eddie Houghton had not taken his drink now and then. There were certain dark rumors in our town to the effect that favored ones who dropped into Kunz's more often than seemed needful were privileged to have a thimbleful of something choice in the prescription room, back of the partition at the rear of the drug store. But that was the most devilish thing that Eddie had ever done.

I don't say that all crews are like that one. Perhaps he was unfortunate in falling in with that one. But it was an Eastern trip, and every port was a Port Said. Eddie Houghton's thoughts were not these men's thoughts; his actions were not their actions, his practices were not their practices. To Eddie Houghton, a Chinese woman in a sampan on the water front at Shanghai was something picturesque; something about which to write home to his mother and to Josie. To those other men she was possible prey.

Those other men saw that he was different, and they pestered him. They ill-treated him when they could, and made his life a hellish thing. Men do those things, and people do not speak of it.

I don't know all the things that he suffered. But in his mind, day by day, grew the great, overwhelming desire to get away from it all—from this horrible life that was such a dreadful mistake. I think that during the long night watches his mind was filled with thoughts of our decent little town—of his mother's kitchen, with its Wednesday and Saturday scent of new-made bread—of the shady front porch, with its purple clematis—of the smooth front yard which it was his Saturday duty to mow that it might be trim and sightly for Sunday—of the boys and girls who used to drop in at the drug store—those clear-eyed, innocently coquettish, giggling, blushing girls in their middy blouses and white skirts, their slender arms and throats browned from tennis and boating, their eyes smiling into his as they sat perched at the fountain after a hot set of tennis—those slim, clean young boys, sun-browned, laughing, their talk all of swimming, and boating, and tennis, and girls.

He did not realize that it was desertion—that thought that grew and grew in his mind. In it there was nothing of faithlessness to his country. He was only trying to be true to himself, and to the things that his mother had taught him. He only knew that he was deadly sick of these sights of disease, and vice. He only knew that he wanted to get away— back to his own decent life with the decent people to whom he belonged. And he went. He went, as a child runs home when it has tripped and fallen in the mud, not dreaming of wrong-doing or punishment.

The first few hundred miles on the train were a dream. But finally Eddie found himself talking to a man—a big, lean, blue-eyed western man, who regarded Eddie with kindly, puzzled eyes. Eddie found himself telling his story in a disjointed, breathless sort of way. When he had finished the man uncrossed his long lean legs, took his pipe out of his mouth, and sat up. There was something of horror in his eyes as he sat, looking at Eddie.

"Why, kid," he said, at last. "You're deserting! You'll get the pen, don't you know that, if they catch you? Where you going?"

"Going!" repeated Eddie. "Going! Why, I'm going home, of course."

"Then I don't see what you're gaining," said the man, "because they'll sure get you there."

Eddie sat staring at the man for a dreadful minute. In that minute the last of his glorious youth, and ambition, and zest of life departed from him.

He got off the train at the next town, and the western man offered him some money, which Eddie declined with all his old-time sweetness of manner. It was rather a large town, with a great many busy people in it. Eddie went to a cheap hotel, and took a room, and sat on the edge of the thin little bed and stared at the carpet. It was a dusty red carpet. In front of the bureau many feet had worn a hole, so that the bare boards showed through, with a tuft of ragged red fringe edging them. Eddie Houghton sat and stared at the worn place with a curiously blank look on his face. He sat and stared and saw many things. He saw his mother, for one thing, sitting on the porch with a gingham apron over her light dress, waiting for him to come home to supper; he saw his own room—a typical boy's room, with camera pictures and blue prints stuck in the sides of the dresser mirror, and the boxing gloves on the wall, and his tennis racquet with one string broken (he had always meant to have that racquet re-strung) and his track shoes, relics of high school days, flung in one corner, and his gay-colored school pennants draped to form a fresco, and the cushion that Josie Morehouse had made for him two years ago, at Christmas time, and the dainty white bedspread that he fussed about because he said it was too sissy for a boy's room—oh, I can't tell you what he saw as he sat and stared at that worn place in the carpet. But pretty soon it began to grow dark, and at last he rose, keeping his fascinated eyes still on the bare spot, walked to the door, opened it, and backed out queerly, still keeping his eyes on the spot.

He was back again in fifteen minutes, with a bottle in his hand. He should have known better than to choose carbolic, being a druggist, but all men are a little mad at such times. He lay down at the edge of the thin little bed that was little more than a pallet, and he turned his face toward the bare spot that could just be seen in the gathering gloom. And when he raised the bottle to his lips the old-time sweetness of his smile illumined his face.

Where the car turns at Eighteenth Street there is a big, glaring billboard poster, showing a group of stalwart young men in white ducks lolling on shores, of tropical splendor, with palms waving overhead, and a glimpse of blue sea in the distance. The wording beneath it runs something like this:

"Young men wanted. An unusual opportunity for travel, education and advancement. Good pay. No expenses."

When I see that sign I think of Eddie Houghton back home. And when I think of Eddie Houghton I see red.